Your Brain's Still Flashing

JIM LIVELY

TREATY OAK PUBLISHERS

PUBLISHER'S NOTE

This is a work of fiction. None of the characters or events is based on actual people, living or dead, or their lives or circumstances. Any similarities are a coincidence and purely unintentional.

**Printed and published in
the United States of America**

TREATY OAK PUBLISHERS

ISBN 978-1-959127-18-5

also by Jim Lively

ABERRANT BEHAVIOR * ARBITRARY AND CAPRICIOUS
CHOKING ON THE SPLINTERS * PUNITIVE DAMAGES
THE PUZZLE AESTHETIC * SURREAL ABSURDITY
NEVER IGNORE MONICA

Available in print and digital on Amazon

DEDICATION

To Fluff, Greta, Frodo,
Jim Bob, Joe Don, P.J. and Monti!

Chapter 1

Simon stood trembling in the reception area of his small office.

This can't be happening! Monica really? I've got to catch up with her. I need answers!

He sprinted across the room to the door that leads to the hallway of the Oak Cliff Bank Tower. His office was located on the second floor just outside of a bank of elevators.

Simon's head jerked back and forth as he scanned the hallway for any sign of Monica. He considered taking the elevator down to the ground floor but knew he could save time by the stairs at the end of the hallway. Simon descended the steps leaping two at a time. He swung open the door on the ground floor foyer just outside of the bank.

Simon shot a glance into the bank's reception area but there was no sign of her inside. He dashed over to the exterior doors and rushed outside to the steps that lead to the sidewalk below. His head rotated back and forth as he scoured the area. A bald thick man dressed in a dark suit was ascending the steps a few feet away.

"Did you see a young brunette woman dressed

in blue jeans and a white shirt exit the building?" Simon shouted.

The man froze and clutched the railing, as if fearful of losing his balance. After a few seconds, he shook his head. "No, you're the only one I've seen exit the building."

Simon darted down the steps past him to the sidewalk which borders Zang Boulevard on the west side of the building. He surveyed the entire area for any sign of Monica.

She can't just have vanished into thin air!

Simon headed toward Jefferson Boulevard, considered the downtown of Oak Cliff where small fifty-year-old retail buildings lined it on both sides. He sprinted two blocks north toward the intersection of Zang Boulevard and Jefferson Boulevard, peering into every car parallel parked along his way.

Monica was nowhere to be seen.

A few yards before he reached the intersection, he bounded west, without looking, across six lanes of traffic. The driver of a red pickup truck southbound on Zang Boulevard laid into his horn as he screeched to a stop with his front bumper just inches from Simon. As Simon reached the other side, a group of people were exiting a drugstore on the corner.

While attempting to skirt around them, his right foot caught the side of a planter box. He lost his balance and crashed face down on the sidewalk pavement.

* * *

Simon sat alone in silence at one end of a table. His eyes darted around, checking out his surroundings. Above him were off-white, drop-down ceiling tiles. Fluorescent lighting illuminated the institutional green walls and dark gray floor tiles. The only furniture in the room was a gray laminated table in the center, surrounded by four matching chairs. In the middle of the table was a silver Sony tape recorder.

I wonder if they're going to record whatever it is that's going to happen here? Hell, I don't even know why I'm here.

Muffled voices came from just outside the door, but Simon could not make out any words. He shifted in his chair, waiting for the door to open. After a few minutes, the voices outside the door went silent. Simon checked his watch and realized he had been waiting for almost thirty minutes.

Why won't someone come here and tell me what's going on?

He shot to his feet and paced the small twelve-by-twelve-foot room. After several trips back and forth, Simon paused next to the door. He grasped the doorknob and attempted to turn it right and then left. It was locked from the outside and did not budge.

Simon let out a heavy sigh, ambled over to his chair, and plopped down. He leaned back and closed his eyes to calm his nerves.

He jolted upright when a small speaker positioned near the ceiling above the door buzzed. He had not noticed it earlier.

A man's deep voice boomed, "Simon, I'll be with you in a few minutes."

Not knowing if the man could also hear him, Simon said, "Why am I locked in here?"

The man's voice cackled. "Why? Do you have some place else you need to be?"

Simon took a deep breath. "No."

"I didn't think so." The man's voice changed to a growl. "Impatience will get you nowhere, Simon."

Simon glanced at his watch. Forty-five minutes had passed. He was about to get up and pace the room again when the doorknob rattled. His eyes were fixed on the door as it swung open.

A large, muscular, bald man dressed in mint green hospital scrubs entered the room and right away closed the door behind him. The man carried a file in his right hand. He marched to the other end of the room and tossed the file on the table. At no time did the man look over at Simon. He flipped through the file. His biceps bulged out from the scrubs.

Simon wondered how he was even able to get his enormous arms through the short sleeves.

After several more minutes passed, Simon blurted out, "May I ask who you are and why I'm here?"

The bald man wore a sneer but did not look up from reading through the file. He flipped through several pages in the file in a methodical manner.

After a few more minutes, he raised his head and glared at Simon. "First of all, I'm the only one asking questions. Is that clear?"

Simon sighed. "Okay."

The man turned on the tape recorder sitting in the middle of the table. "Speak loud enough," he barked, "so the recorder can pick up everything you say, understood?"

Simon nodded. "Yes."

"What's the date?"

Simon sneered. "November 7, 1983."

The man glanced down at the file before him. "How long have you been in this facility?"

Simon shifted in his chair. "About a month."

The man pounded his fist on the table. "You've been here seven weeks and six hours to be precise, correct?"

Simon shrugged. "That sounds about right."

The man glanced back down at the open file. "Do you recall how you got here?"

Simon took a deep breath. "Not exactly. I just remember waking up in a strange room."

The man tapped his large fingers on the desk. "What happened next?"

* * *

As Simon tried to regain his bearings, a woman's voice said, "He's waking up."

Simon's eyes bit by bit focused, and he asked the woman dressed in green scrubs where he was. She didn't answer, so he just lay there staring at the ceiling.

After a few minutes, the door swung open and a man also wearing green scrubs entered the room. He came to the side of Simon's bed. "How are you doing?"

"Who are you?' Simon murmured.

* * *

"Why didn't you answer his question?" barked the man. "Do you like being a rude ass?"

Simon clenched his jaw. He could sense his growing agitation. Why is he being so hostile to me?

He took a deep breath. "I wasn't trying to be difficult. I just didn't know where I was."

The man pounded the table once with his huge fist, his biceps straining at the fabric on his shirt sleeve. "If you didn't know where you were, then why did you ask who the man was?"

Simon sighed. "I thought if he could tell me who he was, then I could deduce where I was. Doesn't that make sense?"

The man rolled his eyes. "Go on with your story."

* * *

"My name is Dr. Stevens and you are an inpatient at Parkland Behavior Health Center. You have been transferred there from the main Parkland Hospital."

"Why did they transfer me to the Behavior Health Center?"

"Someone found you unconscious on the sidewalk and called 911. Do you remember anything about this episode?"

Simon frowned. "I'm not sure now if I dreamed it, but I recall waking up strapped to a gurney in the back of an ambulance. I tried to talk to a man sitting next to me but couldn't get the words out. He stared at me without saying anything. Next thing I remember, I was lying in a cold room, hooked up to an IV and a blood pressure monitor. They ran all kinds of tests on me for several days but couldn't find anything physically wrong with me. After a while, a psychiatrist came into my room and—"

* * *

The man growled, "What was his name?"

Simon glanced up at the ceiling as if that would help him call to mind her name. "It was a woman. I believe her name was Dr. Styers."

"You don't remember?"

Simon shifted in his chair. "I'm certain now that was her name."

The man sighed. "Why did you say you believed her name was Dr. Styers?"

Simon's cheeks blushed as anger churned inside him. "Why are you being so antagonistic toward me?"

"First, I told you at the outset that I'm the only one asking questions. Second, you have no idea how hostile I can be." The man sneered. "Don't try my patience. Tell me about your experience with the psychiatrist."

Simon took a deep breath, struggling to remain calm.

* * *

That day and the next, Dr. Styers asked Simon a myriad of questions. She decided he should be transferred to the Behavior Health Center as an inpatient.

"Can you please tell me why? You're the psychiatrist, so did you ever make a diagnosis?"

Dr. Styers nodded. "Yes, you have symptoms of DID."

Frowning and gasping at the same time, Simon whispered, "And what is DID?"

"DID stands for Dissociative Identity Disorder."

"Can you please describe the symptoms of this..." Simon gulped. "...disorder?"

"A person with this type of disorder can experience such things as hallucinations, anxiety, and multiple personalities."

* * *

The man snapped, "Did you have any of these types of experiences?"

Simon gestured with his head at the file setting on the table in front of the large man. "Isn't that my file there?"

The man sprung to his feet and waved his finger at Simon. "I'm not going to tell you again. I'm the only one asking questions here, comprende?"

Simon's lower lip twitched, which often happened when he was angry. "Okay, I'm sorry."

The man slumped back in his chair.

Simon leaned back and groaned. "Yes, I experienced all three symptoms."

The man leaned forward. "Are you still experiencing them?"

Simon exhaled. "I'm still experiencing anxiety but not the other two symptoms."

The man picked up a piece of paper from the file. "It looks like Dr. Styers has prescribed an anti-depressant and an anti-anxiety medication."

Simon nodded. "Yes, I have been on both drugs for a while."

"Can you be more specific about the time period?"

Simon cocked his head. "One day shy of five weeks for both."

The large man rapped the table with his knuckles. "Why weren't you more specific?"

Simon wrinkled his forehead. "More specific?"

The large man was laser-focused on Simon. "You said you were on both drugs for a while and yet you know the specific time when you started the medications, correct?"

Simon right foot starting bouncing. The man was getting under his skin. "I will try to be more specific in my answers."

The man snickered. "I'm certain you will." He flipped through some papers in the file. "So, you've only experienced anxiety since you have been here.

Any experiences of hallucinations or multiple personalities?"

Simon shook his head. "I haven't experienced either symptom since I have been inpatient."

The large man said, "Tell me about the hallucinations you experienced. When did they first occur?"

"The first time was when I was a junior in college."

"Tell me about it," the man said in a gruff tone, "and be very specific."

Simon's eyes glazed over as he revisited a memory he had long sought to suppress.

* * *

After Political Theory class one day, the girl seated next to Simon introduced herself as Monica. She spoke to him about the subject matter, which was the philosophy of Thomas Hobbes. They had just studied Jean Jacque Rousseau's philosophy earlier.

"Which philosopher do you think was right?" she said, smiling up at him.

Simon stared at Monica. She was beautiful with long brown hair, brown eyes, and pale skin. She wore a light blue shirt and faded blue jeans.

"Thomas Hobbes for sure. What about you?"

Monica winked. "I agree with you."

He gestured with his right hand. "We better get going before the next class starts."

"Where are you headed now?" she said.

"To the Academic Center to study."

"May I join you there?"

"Yes."

Simon tried to concentrate but the lovely girl sitting next to him proved to be a distraction. He glanced over and noticed she was reading the entertainment section of the newspaper.

Monica turned to him and grinned. "Do you like French New Wave movies?"

He nodded. "Absolutely!"

They made a date to go see one that night. While they continued visiting, she told him how much she disliked her insecure roommate.

"How about I'll meet you around 9:30 pm in the lobby of your dormitory?"

Monica winked at him and then shuffled the newspaper.

That night, after Simon waited a bit in the lobby, a girl approached him and told him she was Gweneth, Monica's roommate. Gweneth acted very rude and unpleasant, just as Monica had described her.

"Monica is running late and said you should go ahead and get a seat at the theater where the movie is being screened and she will meet you there."

* * *

Simon paused to collect himself. "Monica never showed up for the film or later for class."

"Did you ever see her again?"

"Not while I was in college."

"What about Gweneth?"

"A few days later, I encountered Gweneth walking with another girl on campus. When I addressed her, she acted as if she had never seen me before. That behavior, coupled with Monica's disappearance, provoked some rage within me. I wanted something bad to happen to Gweneth."

"Did it?"

"A female student committed suicide by jumping off the tower in the middle of campus. What was puzzling is that all the news media identified the victim as Monica Storm and not Gweneth, even though the picture in the media was definitely Gweneth."

"What became of Monica?"

"Not long thereafter, I began to suspect that Monica never existed except in my mind. I used the concept of Monica to provoke me when I needed to be goaded to use telepathy to cause harm to someone."

The man snickered. "That's pretty convenient to have some imaginary person to blame for your actions, isn't it?"

Simon closed his eyes and leaned back. "I suppose so."

"Did Monica ever appear again in a hallucination?"

Simon opened his eyes. "Yes, that's why I'm here." He paused.

"Go ahead with your story. I'm on pins and needles." The man's voice dripped with sarcasm.

Anger churning again inside, Simon gave him a fierce look,. "Why, are you being so insensitive?"

The man leaped to his feet, his nostrils flaring. "What did I say about asking questions?"

Simon was rattled but continued. "Okay, okay."

* * *

One day, Monica showed up in Simon's office. She had not changed in appearance since he first met her in college. She still had long brown hair and brown eyes, and was wearing exactly the same clothes, but he wasn't really certain she was the same girl.

Monica finally gave him enough hints that he figured out who she was.

"But who are you really?"

"I am your dominant personality and you should never ignore me again."

* * *

The man squirmed in his chair. "That's it? She appeared again just so she could reintroduce her old college self to you?"

Simon groaned.

The man rubbed his nose. "Why do you think she reappeared and told you not to ignore her?"

Simon sighed. "I was appointed to represent an indigent client, named Carol Simms in a case where she was charged with felony prostitution. I went above and beyond just representing her in the case because it made me feel better. I—"

"How so?"

Simon leaned forward and rested his elbows on the table. "For example, I gave her money so she wouldn't have to go back to work as a prostitute. Also, I got her an appointment with a social work agency that specialized in helping victims of sex trafficking. She had gotten involved with a terrible man named Frank who was making her work as a prostitute for him."

The man cocked his head. "How did doing these deeds make you feel better?"

Simon shrugged. "I could never fully grasp why, but it lifted some darkness I now attribute to Monica. When I started to be more positive about my life was after I ignored Monica. This is the very strange part. I think Carol and Frank were both hallucinations. Carol just disappeared into thin air."

* * *

After Simon made repeated efforts to call Carol over several days with no answer, he went to her apartment to check on her. Instead, some man and woman lived there, and they didn't know anyone by her name.

"How long have you lived here?"

The man said, "For several years."

One afternoon soon after, Frank confronted Simon with a pistol in the parking garage of his office. "I want Carol's address."

Simon glared at him. His cheeks flushed red with anger. He started trembling and could feel the veins in his neck bulging. "You bastard! Who the hell are you anyway?"

The man started laughing and flexed his muscles. "I bet you'd like to take a swing at me."

Simon sat still, laser-focused on the man.

The man glanced at the ceiling. "What bad event will befall me now? Is that light up there going to come crashing down on my head? What do you see happening to me, Simon? I know I've provoked you. Don't people die when they do something to provoke you? It's all right here in your file. Remember the assistant principal in junior high school, who was smashed under a podium? How about Monica's roommate who jumped off the tower down at UT? You claim to have caused all these deaths, didn't you?"

Simon took several deep breaths and closed his eyes, as a sense of calm swept over him.

The man sank down in the chair. "Simon, tell me what you're feeling."

Simon opened his eyes and stared at the tape recorder. "I don't feel angry anymore. I just feel tired."

The man closed the file in front of him and smiled. "Excellent! To answer your earlier question, I'm Dr. Roberts, a psychiatrist. I specialize in Dissociative Identity Disorders."

Simon cocked his head. "Why were you so hostile to me? Were you testing me?"

Dr. Roberts nodded. "Precisely! I needed to see

how you responded to being provoked."

Simon sighed. "I definitely felt provoked."

Dr. Roberts leaned forward. "But then you calmed down. That's exactly the kind of response I needed to see." He narrowed his eyes. "Simon, do you believe that when you were provoked these other times by people, you were responsible for whatever bad happened to them?"

Simon rubbed a hand through his hair. "I certainly did and to be honest with you, I still do."

Dr. Roberts moved in his chair. "In order to release you from inpatient care, I had to be sure you could control your emotions when you were goaded into becoming angry. Three different psychiatrists have carefully reviewed your case. You have at least two competing personalities. As you are painfully aware, they can pull you in different directions. It is our conclusion that while you may be convinced you have telepathic powers, in fact, they don't exist."

Simon grimaced. "If there had been only one occurrence, then I could possibly be convinced. However, there have been several over the years. A girl in my kindergarten class suffered a severe concussion after she provoked me. That's when I first discovered I had these powers."

Dr. Roberts nodded. "I know, Simon, it's all in your file. The second time you claimed to have used your powers was when a classmate made fun of you in the fifth grade. Of course, then there's the assistant principal in junior high school who humiliated you, and the boorish football player in high school. Don't you think perhaps these all could be just coincidences?"

Simon shrugged. "While I would love nothing better than to think these were mere coincidences, I don't believe they were."

Dr. Roberts sighed, "Well, you don't have to believe it. You have convinced me you can control your anger so you're not a harm to yourself. That's all that's required for you to be released from being inpatient. Should you start experiencing any of these hallucinatory symptoms again, give me a call. We may need to adjust your medication."

Simon forced a smile. "Thank you, doctor."

Chapter 2

Simon took a cab from Parkland back to the Oak Cliff Bank Building where his office was located. He glanced at his watch. It was 2:00 pm, Monday afternoon. Simon took the stairs to the second floor and unlocked the door to his office. It looked the same as it did the day he blacked out several weeks earlier.

As he entered his office from the small reception area, he noticed the light on his answering machine blinking indicating waiting messages. One by one, Simon went through all the messages. Only a handful were from clients. The vast majority were from telemarketers.

At 5:00 pm, he felt exhausted and decided to head home. Simon rode the elevator down to the basement where his car was parked in the garage below the bank. He hoped his old 1966 Pontiac Lemans would start, since it had not been driven the whole time, he was inpatient at Parkland.

When he turned the key in the ignition, the engine groaned.

"Come on, come on!" he muttered, gritting his teeth.

When it at last turned over and started, Simon heaved a sigh of relief. He exited the parking garage and drove a few miles south where he lived in the Wynnewood North neighborhood in the Oak Cliff area of Dallas. He pulled into his driveway.

A stack of newspapers was piled up on the front porch. His mailbox next to the front door was over-flowing with mail. A stack of envelopes and catalogues sat on the red brick planter box that ran down the length of one side of his house.

"The mail carrier must have placed it there when the mailbox got too full."

As he was unlocking his front door, something moved to the left in his peripheral vision. Simon caught a glimpse of a woman in the backyard of the house next door just before she disappeared around the corner.

Wow, that house has been vacant since I moved in a year ago. I wonder if someone has moved in.

* * *

Simon heated up a frozen dinner and decided to watch television while he ate his dinner.

"I'm so relieved to be back in the comfort of my own home." He settled down on the couch and reached for the TV remote.

At 10:00 pm, Simon turned off the television at the conclusion of a rerun of the hour-long drama, Dallas. He switched off the lights in his den and walked over to the window which overlooked the side of his neighbor's house next door.

Simon peered through the venetian blinds at his neighbor's house. None of the windows was illuminated. As he was about to look away, a light switched on in one of the rooms.

I thought that house was still empty. I hope no one has broken in.

The shadow of a woman's figure moved inside the illuminated room just beyond the sheer white window curtains. The figure reached down and picked up an object and held it against her head.

As Simon studied the figure, he could just make out that the woman was holding a phone receiver to her ear.

"Whoever she is, she must have received a telephone call. What is she doing there?"

Simon observed the figure until she set the phone receiver back down. The room at once went dark. He was not certain why, but he continued to stare at the window. The sheer curtains inside the room cracked slightly open. The silhouette of a woman's head peered out.

He snapped his head backwards from the blinds. *Hell, I hope she didn't see me watching her!*

Chapter 3

Simon woke up early Tuesday morning. He decided to head straight to the George Allen Court Building in downtown Dallas. He remembered that almost every morning of the week, the various Dallas County and District Court judges appointed attorneys in criminal cases where the accused was not able to afford to hire an attorney. Although Simon had graduated near the top of his class at Southern Methodist University School of Law, he was not able to land any job offers from the major law firms in Dallas.

The firms were deterred by his unusual quirky personality. He overheard one attorney who interviewed him for a position say to his partner that Simon checked off all the academic requirements but something about his personality was unsettling to him. He had no choice but to go out on his own as sole practitioner. His practice consisted almost exclusively of court appointed cases. While Simon was grateful to receive any type of case, he preferred to be appointed in felony cases tried in the District Courts where the fees for representation were higher.

He wondered if anyone had noticed his absence for

over a month while he was inpatient. Simon entered the courtroom for District Criminal Court 43.

John Smith, a large bald man, was the judge on this court. The judge had appointed Simon to represent numerous clients over the past couple of years.

Simon settled into a seat in the public gallery and watched as attorneys came and went, either filing motions or visiting with the prosecutor about their client's case. He waited, hoping that someone would need his services.

The bailiff glanced down at a piece of paper and called out, "Bill Crawford."

A young man dressed in a work shirt, blue jeans with scruffy dark hair raised his hand.

Judge Smith motioned with his hand. "Approach the bench, Mr. Crawford."

The young man ambled up to the bench. Simon glanced around the courtroom to see if an attorney was going to join him before the Judge.

Judge Smith peered down over his reading glasses at the man. "Do you have counsel, Mr. Crawford?"

Mr. Crawford shook his head. "No sir."

Judge Smith grimaced. "Are you employed?"

"No sir, I got laid off last week."

Judge Smith sighed. "Can you afford legal counsel?"

Mr. Crawford shook his head again. "No sir, I pretty much lived paycheck to paycheck even when I was employed."

Judge Smith narrowed his eyes. "What line of

work were you in?"

"I was a custodian over at the Galleria mall."

Judge Smith scanned the courtroom until he spotted Simon sitting in the gallery. He motioned for the bailiff with his left hand. The bailiff ambled over to the bench.

Judge Smith said, "Go in the hall and see if any attorney out there wants to be appointed to represent an indigent client."

The bailiff hurried down the aisle and exited the courtroom.

Simon's eyes were focused on Judge Smith. A couple of minutes passed before the bailiff re-entered the courtroom, followed by young woman dressed in a white blouse and charcoal gray pantsuit.

The bailiff said, "Judge, this is Ms. Barnett. She's interested in being appointed counsel."

Simon blood boiled. Judge Smith had appointed him as counsel in several cases in the past. *Why didn't he appoint me?*

Judge handed a file down to Ms. Barnett. She and Mr. Crawford walked down the aisle and exited the courtroom.

Simon rose from his seat, entered the bar area, and approached the bench. "Judge Smith."

The judge was flipping through papers in a file. He paused and peered down at Simon. "What can I do for you, Mr. Steed?"

Simon set his briefcase down next to him. "Judge, why didn't you appoint me to represent that client. You saw me sitting out in the gallery."

Judge Smith frowned. "I've heard you had some mental issues. Is that correct?"

Simon sighed. "Yes, I had a breakdown of sorts. But I've received treatment and I'm okay now. I'm desperate to get some appointments so I can get back on my feet."

Judge Smith glared down at Simon. "I'm sure you do, but I'm not convinced you are mentally competent to represent clients. Regardless, my courtroom is not going to be the place where we find out. I recommend you go to the misdemeanor or municipal courts and try to get some appointments. If you prove yourself there, then I will entertain appointing you again as counsel."

Simon's cheeks flushed with anger. He said in a curt tone, "I assure you, I'm mentally competent to represent anyone charged with a crime."

"That may be," Judge Smith growled, "but not in my court!"

Wincing, Simon reached down and grabbed his briefcase and strode down the aisle and exited the courtroom. He visited several other District Criminal Courts. None of them was appointing counsel for indigent clients that morning.

Then Simon drove the short distance back to his office in Oak Cliff. He walked into his office and right away glanced at his voicemail recorder. It was not blinking, which indicated no new messages. He opened a statement from Oak Cliff Bank where he kept his business account. The balance was down to three hundred and fifty-five dollars. That would not be enough to cover a third of his rent.

Hoping his phone would ring, or some prospective client would wander in out of the hallway, Simon remained in his office until 5:00 pm. Frustrated, he grabbed his briefcase and headed home for the evening.

At the last minute, he remembered he did not have any groceries at home and drove to Safeway grocery store inside Wynnewood Village near his home. Simon could not remember how much money he had left in his personal account, so he paid for his groceries out of his business account, further exasperating his business woes.

* * *

That night, Simon sat in his den, fixing a blank stare at his television screen. At the conclusion of the sports on Channel 8., Simon walked across the room and switched off the television. He turned off the lights in the room and wandered over to the window that overlooked the side of his neighbor's house.

Simon peered out between two blinds, careful to stay out of sight. The two rooms next door were illuminated. His eyes darted back and forth between both rooms. Through the sheer curtains, he detected a female figure passing by the window in one of the rooms. That room at once went dark.

His eyes were now focused on the other room. He

watched through the curtains as the female figure picked up the receiver from the phone. A chill shot down his spine as the phone in his kitchen started ringing.

Oh my God, she must have seen me watching her!

Simon went into panic mode. He raced into the kitchen over toward the wall phone. He did not know whether to answer it or not. Simon reached for the phone but paused when it stopped ringing. He reversed course and ran back into his den and peeled open the blinds and peaked out.

His neighbor's house was completely dark. Simon sighed and ambled to the other side of his house where his room was located. He switched off the light, climbed into his bed and closed his eyes.

I have to get assigned a case soon. Otherwise, how am I going to pay my bills?

side of his desk. "Summa Cum Laude from UT, that's impressive, and a law degree from SMU Where did you rank in your law school class?"

He snickered. "I haven't been asked that since I interviewed with law firms after law school. But to answer your question, I graduated in the top five percent."

Her eyes widened. "I suspected as much. I think you should be very qualified to handle my matter. I went to SMU as well and graduated Magna Cum Laude. People with our disorder often are in the top one percentile of the population in intelligence."

Simon raised an eyebrow. "I was not aware of that statistic. May I ask what you did after graduating from SMU?"

"I became a fashion model." Veronica's full red lips twisted into half a smile. "I might add, I had a highly successful career."

His eyes widened. "I'm sure you did. Should we talk about your case?"

She recrossed her legs. "I want to divorce my husband. He's a cheater, dishonest and morally corrupt."

"What's your husband's name?"

"Sterling M. Steele."

Simon scratched on his legal pad. "Can you be more specific as to what he has done?"

Veronica sighed. "Yes, this is one example. We had a huge joint brokerage account at Fidelity. Even though it was funded with the money I made while modeling, he insisted on making it a joint account. Anyway, it was close to a million in assets. I—"

Simon said, "Sorry to interrupt but prior to opening the Fidelity account, where did you have this money?"

"Chase Bank. I kept a separate account there before I was married."

Simon jotted on his legal pad. "When were you married?"

"December 17, 1978."

He leaned forward. "Did you ever commingle the funds you made while modeling with your husband's funds?

Veronica shook her head. "No, he had his separate accounts and I had mine. We kept it that way until we opened the Fidelity account."

"Did your husband put any of his assets into the Fidelity account?"

She glanced upward as if searching for an answer. "I don't think so."

Simon made a note on his legal pad. "Why did you open the Fidelity account in the first place?"

"Sterling is an independent financial advisor." Veronica grimaced. "He pressured me into doing it. I had everything invested at Chase in CDs, a savings account, and checking account. He said I was losing money by keeping it in these conservative investments."

He tapped his pen on the legal pad. "I interrupted you earlier when you said you had close to a million in assets in the account."

She frowned. "I logged into the account a couple of weeks ago and the account was down to around $30,000 in value."

His eyes widened. "What did you do then?"

"Right away I called Sterling and asked what the hell happened to my assets. He got very curt with me and said I authorized the transfer of assets to his bank account so he could invest in a new start-up venture that had a promising future."

"Do you know which bank?"

She sneered. "I'm not sure but I think it's Compass Bank."

Simon jotted on his legal pad. "Do you know the account number."

Veronica shook her head. "No, but I'll try and find out."

He sighed. "Okay, go on with what happened next."

The veins in her neck bulged as she spoke. "I told him I certainly did not authorize any such transfer. That's when he got condescending, attributing my denial to my Dissociative Identity Disorder. I hit the roof. Since I've been in therapy and on medication, I've had no such issues."

Simon said in a gentle tone, "Can you tell me about these issues?"

She reached inside her purse and pulled out a tissue and dabbed her eyes. "I have multiple person-alities. One of my personalities is a spendthrift.

Early in my modeling career, I was spending way more money than I made. It has not manifested itself since I've been married. When we first started getting serious, I made the mistake of telling Sterling. Never did I think he would attempt to use that against me in essence to steal from me."

Simon groaned. "Do you have any other issues with your husband?"

Veronica nodded. "Yes, he's very secretive about where he invests his money. I went through his briefcase one day while he was at the golf course and found several brokerage statements of accounts I never knew existed. When I confronted him about them, he just rolled his eyes and said he was an investment adviser, and those accounts were for clients."

"Did these statements have his name on them?"

She bounced in her chair. "You're damn right they had his name on them. He said he had a power of attorney from his clients to invest in his name."

Simon raised an eyebrow. "That seems a little farfetched."

"Precisely!"

He scratched on his legal pad. "Is there anything else?"

Veronica ran her hand through her hair. "Yes, I'm not one hundred percent certain, but I think he's having an affair. About once every other week, he comes home very late at night. When I ask him where he's been, he always says he was out with the guys."

Simon rubbed his nose. "And you don't believe him?"

She shook her head. "Not with everything else I know about him."

He took a deep breath. "If you want to retain me, I usually charge a $3,000 retainer fee and an hourly rate of $150 when I surpass the amount of the retainer. Is that acceptable to you?"

Veronica fished a checkbook out of her purse and filled out a check. After she signed it, she said, "This is for $5,000. When can you start?" She handed the check to him.

He glanced at it before sliding it into his top drawer. "I can work on the petition this afternoon and file it as early as tomorrow with the District Court."

Her face lit up. "Excellent!"

Simon smiled. "Any other questions at this time?"

"Just one." Veronica leaned back in her chair. "Since you graduated near the top of your law school class, how come you didn't go into a large law firm?"

He sighed. "I interviewed with a number of firms but received no offers. I'm convinced it had to do with my quirky personality, since I suffer from this disorder."

She winked at him. "I happen to think you have a nice personality."

Simon leaned forward. "As you know, however, other personalities are lurking out there."

Veronica raised one eyebrow. "Yes."

* * *

As soon as Veronica left his office, he hurried downstairs to deposit her check into his business checking account.

At least I can pay rent for a couple of months! How much trouble could her divorce proceeding be? It's not like criminal cases. But I can brush up on the law and all the procedures.

Simon took off early and dropped by the butcher on Jefferson Boulevard and picked up a steak. His spirits were elevated for the first time in a long while. As soon as he got home, he set his briefcase down just inside his front door and knelt in front of his stereo console.

After he moved back into his childhood house, Simon had purchased it at a secondhand shop. The console resembled the one his parents owned when he was a child. He even placed it in the same location in the living room where his parents' console had been situated.

Searching for something uplifting, Simon rifled through the stack of vinyl records. He settled on an ancient Kingston Trio record that his older brother used to play when he was very young. It was a live album dating back to the late 1950s entitled, from the Hungry i. Simon knew all the words by heart.

As it rotated on the turntable, the album cracked and popped from years of scratches. He turned the music loud enough so he could hear it all the way down the hallway where his bedroom was located. Simon changed clothes and returned to his living room to listen to the remainder of side 1. He slid into an overstuffed chair he placed in the identical spot where his parents had one many years ago.

Members of the Kingston Trio cracked jokes before every song, which made him smile, even though he had heard the album hundreds of times.

* * *

Simon did his nightly ritual of watching the 10:00 pm news before turning off the television. As he had done every evening since returning home from the hospital, he switched off the den lights and stared through a sliver in the venetian blinds at his neighbor's house.

A light was illuminated in the room where Simon had seen the shadow of a female figure on the telephone through the semi-transparent drapes earlier in the week. He pulled up a chair and decided he would sit there and watch for a while. After all, he had a good day and some money in his business account.

Simon was about to give up and go to bed when the shadow of a female figure appeared in the room. He surmised she had received a call because the figure hurried over to next to the window where he had seen her on the phone last time.

The figure appeared to be pressing the phone receiver next to her ear while the other hand was waving erratically in the air. Simon suspected the phone call must have either excited or agitated the woman. He stared at the silhouetted figure for more than ten minutes.

All of a sudden, the figure slammed down the receiver and hurried across the room. It suddenly went dark. Simon continued to watch his neighbor's house.

In the distance, a dog barked. He wondered if it was the same dog he had heard earlier in the week. As he got up from his chair, a light illuminated the same room of his neighbor's house. Simon was laser focused on the window as the female figure appeared to pick up the phone receiver.

Ten seconds later, he jerked backward as the phone in his kitchen rang. Panting, he sprinted through the darkness of the den and kitchen to where the wall phone was located. Even though it was dark, Simon managed to wrestle the receiver off the phone's cradle on the third ring.

"Hello?"

A voice at the other end of the line whispered, "I warned you before. Quiet your barking dog."

"Wh... who is this?"

The voice growled, "You've been warned."

The dial tone buzzed, signaling the other party had hung up. Simon dropped the receiver and darted back to his den. The receiver bounced below the phone's cradle as it was swung back and forth, scraping against the wall. He eased open a crack in the venetian blinds and peered out. His neighbor's house was completely dark.

That had to be my next door neighbor calling me! But why? I'm going to go over there tomorrow and find out what the hell is going on!

* * *

Simon set the alarm next to his bed and slid under the covers. Over and over, he ran the whole sequence of events involving his neighbor and the phone call through his head.

What if the caller wasn't my neighbor? Regardless, why am I being targeted for a barking dog that's not even remotely close to my house? This is like a nightmare.

Simon dozed off to sleep but was jolted awake at the sound of the phone ringing on the nightstand. He swung his feet out of bed and grabbed the receiver off the phone's cradle on the fourth ring. "Hello."

A man's stern deep voice on the other end of the line said, "Is this Simon Steed?"

Simon cleared his throat. "Uh, yes, I'm Simon Steed."

"Mr. Steed, I'm Sam Pelham, the night clerk at the George Allen Courts Building. We have an arrested suspect who has requested an attorney. Are you available to come down here?"

Simon squinted at the clock. It read 3:00 am.

"Sure, I'll be right down. Where exactly do I go?"

"I'll give your name to the security guard in the lobby. Just show him your bar card and he'll let you go up to the sixth floor."

"Okay, thanks."

In less than ten minutes, Simon slipped on a pair of jeans, a white shirt, and navy-blue sports coat, and was on his way to downtown Dallas. The streets were deserted this early in the morning. He parked parallel next to the George Allen Courts Building.

After a security guard let him inside, he then slipped a key into the elevator, which allowed Simon to access the sixth floor. When he exited, that familiar smell of urine and cleaning chemicals greeted him. He often wondered how the security personnel could tolerate the permeating odor.

A security guard on duty checked his credentials and buzzed him inside. "You here to see Sam?"

Simon nodded. "Yes, Sam Pelham."

The guard gestured to his left with his head. "He's in that office over there."

Simon ambled over a knocked twice on the wooden door.

A man's voice from inside called out, "It's open, come in."

Simon opened the door. Inside a nine-foot by nine-foot room sat Sam Pelham behind a small, laminated plastic desk. He was a short stocky man with a receding hairline. He wore thick horn-rimmed glasses, a wrinkled white shirt, and a red tie that protruded across his bulging belly.

"Mr. Pelham, I'm Simon Steed."

Sam sat reading some paper on his desk. Without looking up, he held up his left hand to acknowledge Simon's presence. After a few more seconds, he glanced upward at Simon and wrinkled his forehead. "Yes, can I help you?"

Simon set his briefcase down next to him. "Yes, I'm the attorney you called about thirty minutes ago."

Sam's eyes lit up as he remembered the phone call. "Yes, I'm afraid you came down here for nothing. The suspect changed his mind and decided to cooperate with the police without having a lawyer."

Simon's eyes narrowed. "Really?"

Sam leaned back in his chair. "Yelp, it happens all the time. But don't worry, you'll still get paid the minimum for your trouble."

"Which is what?"

Sam smiled. "A whopping $500.00."

Simon smirked. "Well, that's better than nothing."

Sam straightened back up and slid a paper across his desk to Simon. "Sign on the dotted line and a check will be in the mail to you within a week."

* * *

Simon drove the short distance back to his home in Oak Cliff. He slowed down to a crawl when he approached his neighbor's house. It was pitch black. To the left, another neighbor's front porch light lit up some of the thirty-year-old cracked driveway leading up to the house.

Simon pulled into his driveway and walked over and unlocked his front door. Once inside, he set down his briefcase and stretched his arms.

Stiff and tired, he trudged into his kitchen, opened the door to his refrigerator, and reached for a can of Coors Light beer. At the last second, Simon changed his mind and slammed the refrigerator door shut. He walked into his dark den and by instinct went over to the window and peered through the venetian blinds at his neighbor's house. It was completely dark.

Why am I becoming so obsessed with my neighbor?

Chapter 6

Friday morning, Simon backed out of his driveway and drove in front of his neighbor's house. He eased by it, checking for any sign of life. All the drapes were drawn, and no car sat parked in the driveway. Simon wanted to stop and knock on the front door but decided instead to go to his office.

He poured his third cup of coffee of the morning and typed a petition for divorce and a restraining order to prevent Veronica's husband from taking any action on financial accounts outside of the normal course of business. Simon wanted to be specific in addressing the Compass Bank account but had to wait for Veronica to find out the account number. He reasoned the general restraining order would put Sterling Steele on notice so he would be hesitant to access the assets for a risky investment venture.

Simon proofread the court filings several times before heading down to the George Allen Courts Building. This was his first-time filing a petition of this nature ever since he clerked for a small firm in his third year in law school.

He managed to get it processed and decided to call it a day at 3:00 pm. Simon was tired from having to get up so early that morning. He arrived home at 3:30 pm, went straight to his kitchen, and fetched a Coors Light beer out of his refrigerator.

Just as he took a huge swig of beer, his doorbell chimed. Simon could not remember the last time anyone had rung his doorbell.

I wonder who the hell that could be?

He dashed across his living room and cracked open the front door.

A heavy-set man, with dark hair, wearing blue jeans and a plaid long sleeve shirt was standing in the center of his front porch. Sitting right next to him on a leash was a beagle.

"Hello," Simon said. "Can I help you?"

"Do you have a problem with my dog?" The man's tone was gruff.

Simon wrinkled his forehead and glanced down at the dog, who started wagging her tail when she made eye contact with him.

"No, you have a beautiful dog. Why would you ask me that?"

"Why the hell do you keep calling me at night to say my dog is bothering you?" the man growled. "You're not even man enough to identify yourself."

Simon's eyes narrowed. "I haven't been calling you."

He thought about telling the man he had also received that kind of phone call but concluded he would not believe him.

Scowling, the man's eyes never left Simon's face.

"I don't believe you. I was in the alley last night and saw you on the phone in your kitchen."

Simon snickered. "I may have been on the phone last night, but that doesn't mean I was calling you. Even if I were calling you, how would you have known, since you were prowling around the alley at the time?"

The man raised his voice. "Because my wife was home at the time and answered the phone. She received a call with that same whispering voice complaining about our dog."

Simon sighed. "So, you were in the alley doing a little investigative work?"

"You're damn right. I may be out there again tonight."

Simon cracked an incredulous smile. "Well, I'll remember to keep my blinds closed then."

The man's face flushed red, as he took a step toward Simon.

Simon held out both hands, palms forward. "Listen, I was just joking. I'm sorry, but I haven't been calling you. I don't even know your name or where you live. By the way, what's your dog's name?"

The man's face softened. "This here's Darcy."

Simon knelt and patted Darcy on the head. "She's beautiful."

"She's a full-blooded beagle."

Simon smiled. "I had a full-blooded beagle when I was a child."

Simon stood back up. He extended his hand

toward the man. "I'm Simon Steed."

"Ted Clements here." The men shook hands.

Simon said, "Nice to meet both you and Darcy. I'm sorry it was under these circumstances."

Ted nodded. "I guess we'll be going."

Simon stood on his porch and watched as they walked down his sidewalk toward the street.

Why would Ted think I was calling about his dog? Wait a minute, he said he saw me on the phone in the kitchen last night. How could he have seen me when the lights were turned off in my whole house?

* * *

Friday night, Simon watched the 1940s horror movie, *The House of Dracula.*

He and his older brother had quarreled all the time. About the only thing they ever agreed upon was to watch the Nightmare Theatre show on their black and white television every Saturday night. The moderator dressed as Count Dracula was featured in a cheap-looking set while introducing the night's horror feature.

It always made Simon nostalgic when he watched these movies as an adult. He had not seen or talked to his brother in years, even though they had spent countless hours in this very den watching television.

The movie concluded at 11:30 pm and Simon switched off the television set and walked over to the window. He cracked open a sliver in the venetian blinds and peeked over at his neighbor's house.

No lights were turned on. Then Simon opened the door from his den to the backyard and surveyed the alley behind his house. He could not see anything in the darkness.

Simon wondered if Ted was roaming the alleys in search of the mysterious caller. He listened intently but could not hear anything. A car eased down the street across the vacant lot behind his house until it disappeared within a few seconds.

Simon locked the door and wandered back to his bedroom. Fatigue from the long day had taken its toll. He fell into bed and pulled the covers tight over him.

Simon jarred awake when the phone on his night-stand rang. He glanced at the alarm clock. It was 1:30 am. Simon debated a few seconds whether to answer it.

He reached for the receiver without getting out of bed. "Hello," he rasped.

A voice at the other end of the line whispered, "Can you hear a dog barking? Of course, you can't. That's what real quiet sounds like."

Simon shouted, "Who the hell is this?"

The voice whispered, "Perhaps you will learn soon enough. Goodnight."

A dial tone sounded. Simon swung out of bed and raced as fast as he could to the den at the other end of his house. He pulled apart the venetian blinds and caught a split-second glimpse of the female figure through the drapes next door before the light in the room was extinguished.

This is just too bizarre! I'm going over tomorrow and meet this neighbor.

As he released the slats of his blinds, Simon heaved a deep breath.

Maybe I should call the police instead.

Chapter 7

Saturday afternoon at 4:00 pm, Simon downed a can of Coors Light beer and felt emboldened. He exited his house through the front door and cut across his neighbor's lawn until he reached the sidewalk. His eyes darted back and forth across the front of the house.

Simon marched up the steps to the front door and rang the doorbell, standing still as it chimed. After waiting a few minutes, he pressed the doorbell button again. No one answered the door.

He decided to go back home. While in route across his neighbor's yard, he scanned each window for any kind of movement but did not detect anything.

Simon entered his house and hurried through his living room to the den. As he had done now on numerous occasions, he slid open the venetian blinds and peered over at his neighbor's house but couldn't see anybody.

Simon retreated to his living room and knelt next to his stereo console. He pulled out the record album, *Their Satanic Majesties Request* by the Rolling Stones from the bin in the console and placed it on the turntable. After several pops and scratches, the first track of the album came to life. Simon hovered over the turntable, mesmerized by watching the album spin. He was jolted back to reality at the sound of his doorbell ringing.

God, I hope that's not Ted Clements again!

Wearing a frown, Simon cracked open the door. Standing on his front porch was a tall, beautiful, pale woman with shoulder length brown hair and piercing green eyes that would rival a Bengal cat. In her late twenties, she wore an untucked long sleeved white dress shirt over faded blue jeans and flats.

Simon's eyes widened when he saw her. He struggled for the words and blurted out, "Hello."

The woman cracked a half smile. "Hello. Did you just come by my house?"

He swallowed. "Uh-huh. Are you my next door neighbor?"

She nodded. "Yes. Did you need to talk to me about something?"

"I didn't think you were home."

The woman narrowed her eyes. "But that doesn't answer my question."

Simon cleared his throat. "I had seen lights on in your house at night, so I thought I would come by and meet you. By the way, I'm Simon Steed."

She gave her hair a flip. "I'm Raven Nevers. I wasn't sure anyone lived here. Have you been out of town?"

He nodded. "Yes, uh-huh, I was out of town for about a month on business. But I've been back all this week."

Raven raised an eyebrow. "Business?"

Simon nodded. "Yes, I'm an attorney."

She looked beyond him into his living room. "Listening to the Stones, I see."

He pushed the door wide open. "Yes, it's on vinyl."

Raven winked. "That's the only way to experience the depth of an album, don't you think?"

His eyes lit up. "Yes, I agree one hundred percent. Would you like to come in?"

She fluttered her eyeslashes. "Sure, just for a few minutes."

He stood to the side to allow her to pass him.

She flounced straight to his stereo console. "How quaint? Your console from the sixties matches the era of the album."

Simon felt his cheeks blush. "I know it's kind of silly, but I grew up with a console like this one."

Raven swept her eyes around the living room. "Judging by your furniture, it appears you enjoy things from another era."

He grimaced. "I guess that's true." He gestured with his hand toward the sofa. "Would you like to sit down?"

She walked over and plopped down on the sofa. He slid into the overstuffed chair.

Simon said, "Have you met many of the neighbors?"

"Your brain's still flashing," Raven said, "like it did when you were young."

His mouth dropped open.

Does she know about my mental issues?

"Excuse me?"

She smiled and pointed over her shoulder with her thumb. "That's the line in the song that's playing now."

Simon bounced in his chair. "Oh yes, of course. I guess I've never paid attention to the lyrics."

Raven squinted at him. "You can't experience the full essence of a song if you don't hear the lyrics."

He shrunk. "I'm sure that's right."

She lightened up. "But to answer your question, I've met just one neighbor, you."

"I've only met a few myself. I haven't lived here long, this time around. I spent the first eleven years of my life in this house. When I saw it listed for sale in the newspaper, I decided to purchase it."

Raven smiled. "You're the nostalgic one, aren't you?"

Simon nodded. "That's true."

I want to ask her about the barking dog.

Instead, he said, "I just met one of our neighbors for the first time yesterday. His name is Ted Clements. He's an interesting fellow with a beautiful beagle dog. I don't suppose you've met him?"

She cocked her head. "No, but what's interesting about him?"

He groaned. "The reason I met him is because he accused me of calling him at night complaining about his barking dog."

She shifted on the sofa. "Did you?"

Simon was laser focused on Raven. "No. In fact,

someone has been calling me to complain about my barking dog. I don't know if the person is a man, a woman, or some kid playing a prank, because they only whisper."

She showed no emotion. "Do you have a dog?"

He shook his head. "Not since when I lived here as a child."

Raven chuckled. "Well, maybe one of your neighbors remembers your dog barking in the night twenty or so years ago."

Simon snickered. "I don't think so. Yet I've heard a dog barking during late hours, but at some distance. I don't know if it belongs to Ted Clements or not. Have you heard it?"

"No." She stood up. "I must be going. Besides, your record is at the end of Side 1. The album was clicking in the dead zone at the end of the album."

She walked over to the console and flipped the album over and set the needle down at the beginning. "There, now you have a fresh side to listen to after I'm gone."

Simon opened the door for her, and she exited his house. He said, "It was nice to meet you."

She bounded down the steps and waved over her shoulder, acknowledging she heard him but did not look around. As she crossed his lawn, he stared until she disappeared around the corner.

What a beautiful but mysterious woman. Does she know I have been watching her through her drapes at night? Is she the person calling about the dog? I just don't know what to think!

Chapter 8

Monday was a cool crisp late November afternoon. Simon stood at the window of his office, gazing down at the trees below. Several of the leaves had already turned a seasonable yellow for the fall.

At the sound of the door opening from the hallway into his small reception area, he turned around and rushed out of his office. A thin man with silver hair, dressed in a Brooks Brothers charcoal gray suit, starched white shirt with pearl cufflinks, red tie and black dress shoes stood just inside the doorway scanning the room.

"Hello," said Simon, "can I help you?"

The man stared a moment at Simon before speaking. "So, this is what a law office looks like in this part of town."

Simon wrinkled his forehead. "What do you mean?"

The man flashed an incredulous smile. "Oak Cliff. I can't say I've ever had the occasion to set foot in any establishment on this side of the Trinity River."

Simon could feel anger stirring inside. "Perhaps you should venture over here more often. You might find it to your liking. Now, is there a reason you're here standing in my reception area?"

The man hurried across the reception area to where Simon stood and extended his right hand, displaying perfectly manicured nails. "I apologize. I see you're a man who likes to get down to business. My name is Rowan Stedman."

After a moment of hesitation, Simon shook hands. "I'm Simon Steed."

Rowan said, "May we sit down?"

Simon gestured with his left hand toward the doorway behind him. "Yes, come have a seat in my office."

Rowan settled into one of Simon's client chairs while Simon plopped down in his desk chair.
He picked up a pen from the top of his desk. "Now, what can I do for you Mr. Stedman?"

Rowan crossed his legs. "You filed a divorce petition and a financial restraining order against my client, Sterling Steele. That's unfortunate."

Simon's eyes narrowed. "How so?"

Rowan chuckled. "For starters, I'm board certified in Family Law with over thirty years of experience in handling these types of cases. You, my friend, are a court appointed criminal defense attorney. On top of that, word has it that you can't even get appointed to those types of cases because of your mental health issues."

Simon felt his cheeks blush with anger. "Get to your point, Stedman."

Rowan uncrossed his legs. "Remember back in law school the first time you got called on by a law professor to answer an impossible question? I certainly remember my first time. I was standing there, scared to death and shaking like a leaf. Anyway, that's how it's going to be for you going against me in court."

Simon sneered at him. "I'll take my chances there."

Rowan shifted in his chair. "There's more. You should be aware that Veronica Steele is not a mentally stable woman. I have no idea what lies she has told you, but they are just that, lies."

Simon sat up straighter. "Well, I've been retained to represent her and that's exactly what I'm going to do. Why the hell did you come over here to Oak Cliff anyway?"

Rowan chuckled. "You haven't met Sadie yet, have you?"

Simon cocked his head. "What are you talking about?"

Rowan waved his hand. "Oh, never mind, I'm just trying to save us all some time and money. Mr. Steele is a reasonable man. If you'll agree to drop the restraining order on his accounts, he will give Veronica a very nice settlement."

Simon bounced his pen on the legal pad in front of him. "How much are we talking here?"

Rowan gazed down at his manicured nails. "He's willing to give Veronica one third of the entire estate plus..." He paused for effect and held up his index finger. "In addition, he's willing to provide Veronica a monthly stipend of $1,000."

Simon sneered at him. "This is a community property state. Unless your client can establish that part of the estate is his separate property, the estate will be divided evenly. That, of course, assumes the divorce was amicable. My client has informed me concerning some of your client's actions that may skew a contested divorce settlement in my client's favor."

Rowan cracked an insincere smile. "And what kind of wild tale did Veronica conjure up this time?"

"That's confidential at the moment," Simon snapped.

Rowan sighed. "The settlement offer remains until one week from today."

Simon shifted in his chair. "I'll pass this information on to my client for her consideration. In the interim, the restraining order remains in effect."

Rowan pushed on the arms of his chair to rise to his feet. "Let me know this week or I will see you in court. By the way, Sterling Steele is a very powerful man in this city. I wouldn't want to get on his bad side."

Simon leaned back in his chair. "Okay. I'll keep that in mind."

Rowan said, "I'll see myself out."

Simon sat still as the door from the reception area to the hallway opened and closed.

He glanced at his watch. It was 4:30 pm. Ten

minutes later, the door to his reception area opened again. Simon assumed Rowan Stedman had returned to make another proposal. He ambled over to the doorway of his office and peered out.

Veronica Steele stood just inside his reception area, staring down at a compact mirror. She was dressed in a navy blue suit, white blouse, matching pumps, and a black Louis Vuitton handbag.

Simon said, "Hello, Veronica."

She looked up from her compact and smiled. "Simon, do you have a few minutes to visit?"

He nodded and stood to the side of the doorway. "Sure, please come in my office."

Simon got a whiff of her perfume as she passed within a few inches of him. Veronica eased delicately into the same chair that Rowan had recently occupied. He was struck by the contrast in appearances of the two.

Simon leaned forward. "Your husband's attorney was just here a few minutes ago."

Her eyes widened. "Really? Rowan Stedman came over to Oak Cliff?"

He chuckled. "Yes, he didn't seem to think too highly of the part of Dallas where I chose to have my law office and I should say also, my home. I'm surprised you didn't run into him leaving the building."

Veronica's face hardened. "He's a snake in the grass. Why did he come here?"

Simon leaned back in his chair. "First and foremost, I think he wanted to intimidate me. He also had a general proposal to settle the divorce."

She raised an eyebrow. "I can't wait to hear what that was all about."

"He offered a third of the entire estate plus a monthly stipend of $1,000."

Veronica cackled. "Are you serious?"

Simon nodded. "Yelp, that was the offer."

She flipped her brunette hair back from her shoulders. "Did you tell him how Sterling ripped off my separate property account?"

"No, but I filed a restraining order along with the divorce decree to keep him from removing any of the estate property for his own investment purposes."

Veronica bounced in her chair. "I bet that got under Sterling's skin."

He picked his pen up off the desk. "Where you able to find your husband's account where he transferred the Fidelity money?"

She nodded. "Yes, I pulled out a Compass deposit slip from his check book that I found in his briefcase. This has got to be the account."

Simon perused the deposit slip. "May I keep this in your file?"

"Of course."

He squinted at her. "Do you and your husband still live in the same house?"

Veronica frowned. "Yes, but our house is very large, and we have separate bedrooms."

"I see."

She leaned forward. "Simon what are the next steps in the divorce?"

Simon twisted the pen around his fingers. "We'll go through the discovery phase so we can get a handle on all the assets. Depending upon what motions, if any, Rowan Stedman files on behalf of your husband, we may have a hearing or two before we go to court to prove our case."

Veronica stared at him as if to help her process what he just said. "How long will all this take?"

He grimaced. "It might take up to a year."

"What will I do about my living expenses until the divorce if finalized?"

"You're permitted to withdraw what you would normally do. You don't have to change your lifestyle but just don't make any extraordinary withdrawals or do anything financially that would raise suspicion."

She exhaled. "That's a relief."

Simon stared down at his legal pad. "When we first met, you said you thought your husband might be having an affair. Do you have any further information that may substantiate your concerns? Since the divorce is contested, his infidelity could factor into your share of the estate."

Veronica fished in her handbag and pulled out a book of matches. "Just this." She handed them to Simon.

He studied the cover for a few seconds. "Park Cities Social?"

"It's an exclusive private dinner and night club in

the Park Cities."

Simon flipped open the cover. Written on the inside was a notation and he read it out loud. "Margot 214.542.5159."

He looked up. "Do you know this person?"

She shrugged. "No. I'm pretty sure no one by that name is a member there."

Simon studied her face. "Why do you think this is suspicious then?"

Veronica frowned. "I found it in his suit coat pocket the next morning after one of his late nights, supposedly out with the boys."

His eyes widened. "I see. Did you call the phone number by the name?"

She shook her head. "No, I was hoping you would investigate and find out about this woman."

He sighed. "Veronica, that's really kind of a Perry Mason thing you see on television. Attorneys don't do that in real life. You might be better served hiring a private eye to do the investigation. His or her hourly fee would be much less than mine."

Veronica pursed her lips. "Money is no object. I trust you and want you to see what you can find out about Margo."

Simon cocked his head. "Very well. I'll see what I can turn up. You said you didn't think Margo was a member of the club. Is there a membership list or some way to verify if she's a member?"

She nodded. "Yes, I can get a list of the members."

He leaned forward. "Is it possible that Margo may

work at Park Cities Social?"

"I suppose."

Simon rubbed his nose. "Are non-members ever allowed inside?"

Veronica flipped her hair. "Only if accompanied by a member."

"Is there a way that you can get me inside?"

She cracked a smile. "Yes, I can take you as my guest to dinner tonight. My husband's out of town on business."

He raised an eyebrow. "That still sounds risky. Are you sure you wouldn't want to do this part alone?"

"I'm positive. If Margo does work there, she might know I'm Sterling's wife. I want to catch her by surprise."

Simon tapped his desk with a pen. "It's possible Margot doesn't work there, and your husband just used the club's matches to make a note. Does your husband smoke?"

Veronica shook her head. "No, so why would he need to carry matches around in his coat pocket?"

"Hopefully, we will find out. What time did you want to go this evening."

She looked at her watch. "Let's meet at Park Cities Social at 6:45 pm. I'll wait for you near the elevators in the lobby of the building. The address is on the book of matches."

He glanced down at the book of matches. "Okay, I'll be there."

Chapter 9

At 6:30 pm, Simon eased his 1966 Pontiac Lemans into the parking lot next to the office building where the Park Cities Social was located on the 15th floor. He parked between a brand-new black Mercedes 380 SL and a sleek white Corvette 350. Before turning off the ignition, he surveyed the parking lot. It was filled with upper-end, late-model luxury cars.

Judging by the cars parked here, I must be in the right place.

He opened the door which led to the lobby and right away spotted Veronica standing near a bank of elevators. She had changed clothes, now wearing a black dress, with matching pumps and handbag.

Simon could not help but think how striking she appeared. He surmised that except for a few age-appropriate wrinkles, she probably did not look much different than when she was a model.

She flashed a smile when she saw him and gave him a slight wave with her right hand. "You're right on time."

Simon smiled. "If nothing else, I'm punctual."

They rode the elevator up to the 15th floor. When

the doors opened, a man in a dark suit, white shirt, and gray tie greeted them.

"Good evening, Mrs. Steele. I understand you will be dining with us this evening."

Veronica raised her chin in an act of superiority. "Yes, Daniel. My guest and I would like to sit at my usual table next to the windows."

Daniel bowed. "Right this way."

Simon followed Daniel and Veronica into the dining room. At least half of the tables were occupied. Simon felt as if all eyes were focused on him with fierce intensity.

Maybe it's a Park Cities Social thing to eye any non-member. On the other hand, maybe they're all staring because they're wondering why Veronica is dining alone with a strange man.

He was relieved when they were at last seated at their table.

During dinner, Veronica said, "Do you mind sharing a little bit about what you experienced with your Dissociative Identity Disorder?"

He sighed. "Yes, at an early age I discovered I had these strange powers. At least, they were very real to me. If people did something to make me very angry, horrid things would happen to them. In college, I met this beautiful girl named Monica. We had a date to go to a movie. She never showed up then or ever again. Over time, I began to think that she was just a figment of my imagination. I thought of her when I was provoked by someone. Just over a month ago, Monica showed up one day in my office. She had not changed in appearance since college. I had been representing a woman in a prostitution case who I took a personal interest in helping her get her life back in order. Monica informed me that she was my dominant personality and that she did not approve of my helping this person and ignoring her. Next thing I knew, I woke up at Parkland hospital."

Veronica appeared to be concentrating on his face as he spoke. "What kind of things provoked you?"

He took a sip of wine. "Childish things when I was a kid, such as some kid making fun of me because he was named a school safety patrol, and I wasn't."

She leaned close to him. "What happened to him?"

"He fell from some exercise bars in the gymnasium and crashed to the wood floor below."

Her eyes widened. "And you thought you caused it?"

Simon grimaced. "I'm convinced I did."

"What about as an adult?"

He took another sip of wine. "As an adult, something as meaningless as someone's stupidity could provoke me."

Veronica reached over and patted his hand. "Give me an example."

Simon pursed his lips. "I was appointed to represent a guy, named Jackie Wayne Timmons. He was charged with murder. Jackie was a flight risk, so I had to meet him in one of the interview rooms at the county jail. This guy obviously had some severe mental issues."

He stopped talking until Veronica said, "Go on."

"I asked him if he would agree to being examined by a psychiatrist. It was the only hope I had in creating some kind of defense for him. Jackie emphatically refused. Before the guard came to escort him back to his cell, I told him to be careful because the guard's pistol was not properly secured in his holster."

Simon paused and took a drink of water. "After the guard left the room with him, I remember saying under my breath, now Jackie. That's when I heard a scuffle just outside the door and then a gunshot. When I cracked open the door, Jackie was lying face down in a pool of blood."

She cocked her head. "It sounds like all you did was just plant the idea and Jackie acted independently upon it."

He frowned. "No, I knew it was going to happen. You can imagine, though, how the doctors weren't convinced I was the perpetrator."

Veronica nodded. "Yes, but my sister was convinced, and she spent a great deal of time on your case."

Simon forced a smile. "Yes, she did."

She leaned closer and placed her hand on top of his hand. "Do you think you could possibly be provoked again into killing someone?"

He let out a long heavy sigh. "Yes, if the circumstances were right. Before I was discharged from the hospital, I was isolated in a small room, not knowing what was going to happen. Finally, this muscular doctor came in and began drilling me with a barrage of questions. He kept this up what seemed like an eternity constantly interrupting and challenging me. This was the final test to see if I could be goaded into doing some catastrophic. The doctor was satisfied that all these telepathic powers I claimed to possess were all in my mind. I was discharged that afternoon."

Veronica was keenly focused on him and appeared to hang onto his every word. "But you weren't convinced?

Simon shook his head. "Not one bit. I know I possess these powers."

"Did you share these feelings with that doctor?"

He nodded. "Yes, but he was satisfied with the opinions of the other psychiatrists who said it was all mental and I had no such powers."

She snatched her hand from on top of his and straightened up in her chair. Simon glanced up as a short rotund bald man, dressed in a light gray suit, white shirt, and red tie which matched the color of his cheeks, approached their table. He said, "Veronica, I thought I saw you come in earlier."

Veronica cracked a slight smile. "Oh, hi, Tom. How's Linda?"

He chuckled. "Linda's doing fine. She's out with the girls."

The man then shifted his gaze to Simon. "Tom Williams here."

Simon shot to his feet. "Simon Steed."

Veronica jerked her head toward Simon. "Simon's my attorney."

Tom's left eyebrow arched. "Really? Speaking of attorneys, I saw your husband having dinner with Rowan Stedman just last week."

She stared expressionless at Tom and without emotion said, "Sterling and I are getting a divorce."

Tom's mouth dropped open. "I'm sorry, Veronica. I didn't know. You make such a wonderful couple." He coughed. "Well, excuse me. I'll leave you two alone."

They both watched as Tom waddled his way across the dining room and out the door.

After dinner, the server cleared their dishes. She said, "I'm going to go powder my nose. I want you to go into the bar and see if you can find out if Margot works here or anything else about her."

He smiled. "Of course. Just point me in the right direction."

Veronica jerked her head sideways. "It's just out that door and down the hallway on the right."

"Are you going to join me there later?"

She shook her head. "No, I don't want to be seen there since you will be inquiring about this woman. I'll wait for you in the lobby downstairs. When you get the bill, just write my last name and number 2769. Sign it illegibly."

Simon snickered. "That won't be hard, with my bad handwriting."

They parted company in the hallway, and he entered the bar. Simon paused just inside to get his bearings.

The bar, although dimly lit, had polished hardwood floors and rich wood paneled walls. The tables were about a third occupied, primarily by men. He approached an ornate wood bar. It was empty except for two men perched at the end to his left. Simon took a seat three stools in from the other side.

As soon as he was situated, a tall, thin, blond woman dressed in white blouse and black slacks approached him from behind the bar. She smiled. "May I get you something to drink?"

Simon rested his elbows on the bar. "Citron Vodka and soda, please."

He watched as she made his drink and set it on a cocktail napkin in front of him.

The woman said, "Did you want to start a tab?"

"No, I'll just have this one."

She placed the bill in a leather sleeve and paused and stared at him. "I don't think I've seen you in here before. Are you a new member?"

Simon shook his head. "No, I'm a guest of the Steeles."

The woman set the bill next to his cocktail. "I haven't seen Mr. Steele in here for a few days."

He shifted on the stool. "Does he come here often?"

She nodded. "Yes, he's usually with some woman. Wait a second, you said 'Steeles'. He's not married, is he?"

Simon nodded. "Yes, there's a Mrs. Steele."

Her face at once contorted. "I'm so sorry. I shouldn't have said anything personal about Mr. Steele."

He smiled. "I assure you, it's quite all right. By the way, I'm Simon."

The woman's face softened. "I'm Deloris. Nice to meet you."

"Nice to meet you, Deloris. Do you by any chance know a friend of Mr. Steele named Margot?"

She shrugged. "That could be one of the women he brings in here, but I can't say for sure."

Simon leaned forward. "Does anyone named Margot possibly work here?"

Deloris shook her head. "Not to my knowledge."

He took a sip from his drink. "Thanks, Deloris."

Simon finished his drink and signed the tab as Veronica had instructed.

He took the elevator down to the lobby. When the door opened, Veronica was pacing back and forth across the empty lobby. She rushed over to him.

"Did you find anything out about Margot?"

Simon shook his head. "No, but I did find out some interesting things about your husband."

Her eyes widened. "Really?"

"I spoke with the bartender named Deloris. She didn't know your husband was married. According to her, he has brought several different women into the bar in the past."

Veronica's face hardened. "I knew it! That bastard!"

He rubbed his chin. "When I asked if one of the women could've possibly been named Margot, she didn't rule it out but didn't know. She also said to her knowledge, no one by that name works at Park Cities Social."

Veronica frowned. "I guess that's a dead end then."

"Not necessarily. I can still call the number on the match box."

"Now you see what I have had to put up with in this marriage." She grabbed his arm. "Shall we go?"

* * *

Simon opened the front door to his house as his phone was ringing. He sprinted through his dark living room to his kitchen. He rubbed his palm up and down the wall just inside the entrance in search of the light switched.

Just as he was able to flip it on, the phone stopped ringing. He turned the light back off and made his way through the kitchen to the den.

Simon darted over to the window and peered out at his neighbor's house between a crack in the venetian blinds. He arrived just in time to see the lights switched off next door.

I wonder if my neighbor Raven was trying to call me? I hope it's not another neighbor.

Chapter 10

Tuesday afternoon, Simon opened the file he had created for Veronica Steele's case and fished out the matchbox. He stared at the phone number on the inside cover a few seconds before he reached over and grabbed the phone receiver. Simon picked up a pen off his desk as he was listening to the phone ring on the other end of the line.

On the third ring, a woman's voice said, "Hello."

In a friendly tone, Simon said, "Hello, is this by any chance Margot."

After a pause at the other end of the line, the woman said. "Who wants to know?"

He thought the voice sounded vaguely familiar. "Simon Steed. I'm an attorney."

The voice at the other end snapped, "What do you want?"

"I'm following up on a lead for a client. Are you acquainted with Sterling Steele?"

Simon thought he heard a sigh from the other end of the line.

"What if I am? I didn't do anything wrong."

He jotted on his legal pad. "No one is accusing you of doing anything wrong. I'm just trying to find out about your relationship with Mr. Steele."

The voice at the other end hissed, "Why don't you call Sterling and ask him?"

Simon growled, "I would do that if I could, but I can't"

"Why the hell not?"

He gripped the pen tightly with his right hand. "Because I represent his wife, Veronica Steele."

Simon heard what he thought was a gasp at the other end of the line.

"What are you trying to pull? Sterling is not married."

He jotted on his legal pad. "Is that what he told you?"

The voice at the other end of the line screamed, "Go to hell, you bastard."

The dial tone sounded, and Simon dropped the receiver back onto the phone's cradle.

Sterling Steele is morally bankrupt. I have even more sympathy for Veronica. Where have I heard that woman's voice before?

The door from the hallway to his office reception area opened. Simon pondered who entered his office and made his way over to the door.

A rough-looking man with slicked back black hair and dark eyes, wearing a charcoal gray suit, black tie, and white shirt, stood in the middle of the reception. He stared straight ahead.

Simon said, "Hello, can I help you?"

The man shifted his eyes to focus on Simon and

said in a gruff tone, "You the attorney Simon Steed?"

Frowning, Simon narrowed his eyes. "Yes, I'm him. What can I do for you."

"We need to talk."

Simon grimaced. "Who exactly are you?"

"Boris Denucci," the man barked.

Simon cocked his head. "Do I know you?"

Boris shook his head. "No, I'm a friend of the Steeles."

"Well, okay, I have a few minutes available." Simon gestured with his head toward his office. "Let's go in my office."

He stood to the side of the doorway to let Boris enter first. The man slid into one of the client chairs and Simon hurried behind his desk and plopped down in his chair. Having the desk separate the two of them gave Simon a bit of comfort.

Boris unbuttoned his suit jacket which revealed a glimpse of a black pistol holster. Simon's eyes widened.

Boris cleared his throat. "It's in the best interests of everyone involved that the Steele divorce ends quickly and amicably."

Simon stiffened in his chair. "You say you're a friend of the Steeles. Does Mrs. Steele know you're here?"

Boris cracked an incredulous smile. "That's irrelevant. The only thing that matters is that you do your part to get this whole divorce over as soon as possible. The offer that Rowan Stedman made on behalf of Mr. Steele is more than fair. You need to convince Veronica Steele to accept his offer."

Simon sighed, "My job is to represent my client's best interests and that's exactly what I intend to do. I'm not going to be intimidated and pressured into doing something unethical as what you propose."

Boris stared at him for several seconds before rising to his feet. He buttoned his suit jacket and patted the bulge created over the gun holster. "You're making a mistake. I don't have a chance to get over to Oak Cliff very often. I hope it's safe over here because I suspect I'll be back soon."

He turned and walked briskly out of the office. Simon rushed over to the doorway and watched as Boris exited the reception area into the hallway. He wiped beads of sweat off his forehead with his shirt sleeve. He was both nervous and furious at what had just transpired. He had not had this dark emotion since he had received therapy and medication at Parkland Behavioral Health Center.

Simon sat back down behind his desk and closed his eyes.

This Sterling Steele is a monster! I want to more than punish him financially!

He jerked upright when his phone rang. Simon picked it up on the third ring.

"Hello, this Simon Steed."

A woman's voice at the other end said, "Oh, Simon, I'm glad I caught you before you left for the day. This is Veronica."

He exhaled. "Hello, Veronica. How are you doing?"

"I'm okay. I wanted to see if you were available to meet for dinner tonight?"

His mouth dropped open. "I... I suppose so."

"Have you heard of Routh Street Café? It's a new restaurant that's getting rave reviews."

"Yes, I've read something about it in D Magazine."

"I made us reservations at 7:30 pm. I thought we could discuss my case."

Simon rested his elbows on his desk. "Well, there have been a few developments since we last talked."

"Excellent, I'll see you then. Bye Simon."

"Goodbye, Veronica."

He hung up the phone and stared at it for a few moments.

Why does she want to have dinner with me again? This case is getting stranger by the day!

* * *

Routh Street Café was a two-story structure located in a transitioning part of Dallas just northwest of downtown. Antique stores, a couple of art galleries and an occasional bar occupied the surrounding area.

Simon steered his old Pontiac Lemans into an empty parking space a block away. What few businesses in the immediate area were shuttered for the night. He ambled up the cracked sidewalk until he reached the entrance to the restaurant. Simon opened the door and was gasped at the scene inside.

The old building had been completely updated inside and offered a contemporary vibe. Well-heeled patrons swarmed around the bar to his right. Simon was about to approach a man perched behind a podium he presumed to be the host when someone tugged his sleeve and a woman's voice said, "Right on time, as always."

Veronica stood there, smiling at him. She was dressed in a black dress with a matching Prada handbag and pumps.

He bowed his head. "One of my few good traits."

"I'm sure you have more than a few good traits." She winked at him. "Let's be seated at our table."

The two of them followed the host over to a table away from the bar area. Veronica said, "I asked for a quiet table so we could talk."

They dined on Southwestern cuisine that was a specialty of up-and-coming chef, Stephan Pyles.

Veronica said, "You mentioned some new developments in my case?"

He nodded and set down his glass of chardonnay. "Yes, first I called the number on the matchbox and a woman answered. I asked if she was Margot. She never did admit to being her. She was more intent on trying to find out who I was. She did acknowledge knowing your husband. I couldn't get any real details about their relationship. There were a couple of interesting things, though."

Veronica was laser focused on Simon. "What was that?"

He sighed. "She seemed surprised to learn Sterling was married. In fact, she was emphatic that Sterling was *not* married. When I assured her, he indeed was married, she hung up the phone."

The veins bulged in Veronica's neck. "That sorry bastard!"

Simon smirked. "That's what she called me before she hung up."

Veronica frowned, trembling as she spoke. "You see why my life has been a living hell?"

"Yes, Sterling Steele is piece of work. We're going to take him to the cleaners."

Veronica reached over and patted his arm. "I'm glad I hired you as an attorney." She paused and rubbed her chin. "You said there were a couple of interesting things about your conversation. What was the other thing?"

He cocked his head. "It was very strange, but I think I recognized the woman's voice from somewhere."

She wrinkled her forehead. "Where could you have possibly heard her voice before?"

Simon shrugged, "I don't know. I just can't quite place where I heard it before."

"Could she have been a client of yours?"

Simon shook his head. "I don't think so."

Veronica took a sip of wine. "Any other developments with my case?"

He shifted in his chair. "Yes, I had an interesting visitor this afternoon."

She leaned closer to him. "Oh really, somebody came to your office about my case?"

Simon nodded. "Yep, he said his name was Boris Denucci. This guy was a character straight out of the gangster movies, right down to his pistol and holster."

Veronica's mouth dropped open. "He had a gun?"

"Yes, he never pulled it out of his shoulder holster, but he made damn sure I knew he carried one."

She patted his hand. "Oh my! What did he want?"

Simon sighed. "He said he was a friend of you and your husband. Have you ever met him?"

With growing vigor, Veronica shook her head. "No, never!"

"That's what I thought. Anyway, he said it was in everybody's interest that this divorce gets amicably resolved as soon as possible."

"What's that supposed to mean?"

Simon picked up his wine glass and stared at it before taking a final sip. "He wanted me to convince you to take the settlement offer made by your husband's attorney. I told him I wouldn't do that, and I was going to represent your interests to the best of my ability. Obviously, Mr. Denucci didn't care too much for my response and told me I was making a mistake. He stood up, patted his coat pocket where his pistol was holstered and made a thinly veiled threat that he would be spending more time in Oak Cliff."

She grabbed his arm. "That's horrific! Weren't you scared?"

He nodded. "Yes, and angry as well. I haven't had those dark feelings since being on medication."

Her eyes lit up. "Do you think you could have been provoked enough to make something bad happen to him?"

Simon stared ahead. "Yes, I think so. I've never met your husband, but I think he's abominable!"

Veronica squeezed his arm. "He's the worst, Simon. I hate him so much! I just wish he would vanish off the face of the earth!"

He took a deep breath to compose himself. "Let's work on getting as much of the estate as possible for you."

She released his arm. "I'm so glad I retained you as my attorney."

* * *

As Simon drove home from dinner, he kept replaying the whole evening through his head. *Veronica sure looked beautiful tonight! How could her husband treat her so badly? I get angrier and angrier, the more I learn about him!*

As Simon pulled his Pontiac into the driveway, he thought that he had caught a glimpse of someone on his front porch. He was not certain because it was dark, and his porch light was not turned on.

Simon turned the ignition off and eased out of his car. He walked over the lawn to his front porch. The whole porch was not visible because of the tall gardenia bushes that lined that side of his house. Simon had intended to trim them several times a couple of weeks ago but procrastinated each time.

As he rounded the final bush, he flinched as he spotted a figure standing next to the front door.

A woman's voice said, "Did I startle you?" When the figure took a few steps toward him on the porch, Simon recognized his neighbor, Raven.

"Raven, is that you?"

As she drew nearer, he could make out her attractive features.

"Yes, I was wondering when you were going to get home."

Simon wrinkled his forehead. "Is everything okay?"

She smiled. "Of course."

He fished his keys out of his pants' pocket. "Uh, would you like to come in?"

Raven nodded. "Sure, just for a moment."

Simon fumbled with the lock for several seconds but managed to get the door open. Once inside he switched on the living room lights.

Raven's brown hair was pulled back in a ponytail. She was dressed in faded jeans and a simple white blouse.

He said, "Can I offer you something to drink?"

She shook her head. "No, thank you. I just came by to tell you that some man was looking for you earlier in the evening."

He raised an eyebrow. "Really? How do you know?"

"I was driving home just before dark. As I passed your house, I saw a man standing on your front porch. First, he rang your doorbell and then knocked on the door. I stopped my car in front of your house since I didn't recognize him. A few seconds later, he walked over to the window and attempted to peer inside through a crack in your living room drapes. I think he saw me watching him, so he walked around to the side of your house and disappeared. I drove home and went inside. Several times I looked out of both of my bedroom windows, but never saw him again. Since he was so suspicious acting, I thought I should come over and tell you."

Simon was focused on her, hanging on every word. "Thank you, I appreciate that very much."

She glanced over at the sofa. "May I sit down?"

He nodded. "Of course."

Graceful and confident, Raven perched at the end of the sofa. Once settled, she patted the cushion next to her. "Come and sit down. It looks like you've had a hard day."

He plopped down on the sofa a few feet away from her. "It was an interesting day for sure."

She glanced at her watch. "Since it's already after 9 pm, it was also a long day for you."

He leaned back on the sofa. "I was out to dinner with a client."

"Where did you and he go?"

Simon cracked a slight smile. "Actually, my client's a woman. I'm representing her in a messy divorce. We went to Routh Street Café."

Her eyes lit up. "I've heard about that restaurant. I've been wanting to go there."

"It's very nice."

Raven's face hardened. "You said this is a messy divorce?"

He nodded. "My client's husband sounds like a real jerk. I don't blame her for divorcing him."

She leaned near him. "What's your client like?"

"My client's a former model. She's extremely attractive and seems nice. I can't really be more specific without going into her case."

Raven smiled. "I understand." She brushed his leg with her hand. She scooted to the edge of the sofa. "Well, I better be going."

"Of course." Simon shot to his feet. He opened the front door and she exited.

As she passed him in the doorway, Simon said, "Oh, wait, I almost forgot to ask you. What did the man look like who was hanging around my house?"

"It was dusk so I couldn't get a good look at him. But he was stout, had dark hair, and dressed in a suit."

Simon grimaced. "I wonder who he could be?"

Raven stepped off the porch onto the sidewalk. Without looking around said, "Good night, Simon."

"Good night and thanks again."

She waved her hand, acknowledging she had heard him.

Simon went into his den and flipped the television

on to watch the last part of a sitcom on Channel 8.

After the news, he performed his nightly ritual of turning off the television and peering out a crack in the venetian blinds at his neighbor's house. No lights were illuminated in either bedroom that faced his house.

He ambled to the other end of his house and prepared for bed. As soon as he switched off the lamp on his nightstand, a chill shot down his spine.

Was Boris Denucci the stranger hanging around my house, paying me a visit?

Chapter 11

Wednesday morning at 9:00 am., a courier delivered a notice to Simon's office notifying him of a hearing the following Monday at 10:00 am. Rowan Stedman had filed a motion challenging the restraining order on Sterling Steele's accounts.

Simon recalled from law school that a party had to give a minimum of three days' notice before a hearing could be scheduled. Rowan Stedman had given him the minimum amount of time to prepare.

What do I need to do to get ready? I haven't studied Family Law since law school. I have to do some research and in a hurry!

Simon grabbed his briefcase and took the stairs down to the basement parking garage of Oak Cliff Bank where his Pontiac was parked. In a matter of minutes, he was driving north on the Central Expressway. He exited at Mockingbird Lane and drove east toward the south side of Southern Methodist University. Simon took a right on Hillcrest and parked in a residential area just north of campus.

He had not been back to campus since he graduated from law school five years ago. The scene in the law school quadrangle had not seemed to change since then except the students appeared younger. He spent a couple of hours researching restraining orders and other aspects of trying a divorce case in Texas. Since he had only handled criminal law cases after graduation, he felt unprepared for the hearing on Monday.

Simon jotted down a rough draft of a *subpoena duces tecum*, which would require Sterling Steele to provide documentation of all activity on all his financial accounts from the date the restraining order went into effect, prior to the hearing. He wanted to determine if Sterling Steele had complied with the terms of the restraining order.

After remembering the library offered several small rooms with typewriters available for students to use as needed, Simon took the elevator up to the top floor. He located an empty room and quickly typed the subpoena duces tecum. He proofread it and hurried back down to the ground floor and exited the library.

Simon sped to the George Allen Courts Building. He was determined to get it filed that afternoon in ample time to have it served on Sterling Steele prior to the hearing. The clerk date stamped his *subpoena duces tecum* which indicated it would be served not later than Friday. Then Simon drove back to his office in Oak Cliff.

His office phone was ringing when he entered his reception area from the hallway. He sprinted to his office and grabbed the receiver off the phone's cradle. "Hello, this is Simon Steed."

"Oh Simon, I've been trying to get a hold of you. This is Veronica Steele."

He slid into his office chair. "Hello, Veronica, I was going to call you in the morning."

"Do you know anything about this hearing scheduled for Monday?"

Simon thought he detected a tenseness in her voice. "Yes, I received notice of it today myself."

She sighed. "It looks like they're trying to get the restraining order removed. What are you going to do about that?"

He leaned back in his chair. "I did research this afternoon on your case and prepared a *subpoena duces tecum* to be served on your husband prior to the hearing."

"What the hell is that?"

Simon twisted a pen in his hand. "It's a subpoena that will compel your husband to provide documentation of all activity in his financial accounts. Unless your husband can establish some compelling evidence why the restraining order should be lifted, the judge will most likely keep it in place until your divorce is finalized. I believe Rowan Stedman is trying to intimate us. I need to be prepared for anything, so that's why I want to review the account activity."

He thought he heard Veronica exhale before she said, "Okay, that's good. Do I have to appear at the hearing?"

"No, not if you don't want to. I would like to meet with you this weekend, if possible, to go over the accounts, assuming we get the documents requested."

"Of course. Just let me know when and where you would like to meet."

"Will do, goodbye, Veronica.

Chapter 12

Thursday morning, Simon arrived at the George Allen Courts Building promptly at 8:00 am. One of his clients he obtained from the graveyard shift had his first appearance in Judge Bonham's court. He had not been back to this courtroom since he was informed by Judge Bonham that no judge would appoint him to represent any indigent clients because of his mental issues.

Simon wondered how Bonham would react to him. He opted to wait for his client on one of the benches in the hallway just outside the courtroom. Simon spotted his client, Jack Stoddard, as he stepped off the elevator. Jack was a slender, middle-aged man with salt-and-pepper thinning hair. He was dressed in blue jeans and a denim work shirt.

Simon waved him over to the bench where he was sitting. "Let's visit here a few minutes before we go inside for your plea."

Jack sat down. "How long will this take?"

Simon leaned forward. "Probably just a few minutes. Now let's go over what we discussed. As you know, the police botched your Miranda warning. The prosecutor offered to let you plea to a lesser offence.

As you also know, I've advised you to plea 'not guilty' because the whole case should be thrown out. They don't have any evidence other than what you told them."

Jack nodded. "I know, man. I'm going to do what you told me to do."

"The judge may ask some questions about the case. If he does, I can bring up the botched Miranda warning. Don't speak unless the judge asks you a question. Are you ready to go inside the courtroom?"

Jack stood up. "Let's do it."

Simon and Jack sat side by side in the front row of the public gallery until the bailiff called out Jack's name. Janet Weiss was the prosecutor assigned to the case. She was an early-thirties blond woman dressed in a navy blue pant suit and a coordinating light blue blouse.

Judge Bonham did not look up until all parties stood before him. He glanced down at them over his reading glasses. Simon thought he detected a slight smile from the judge when they made eye contact. Judge Bonham said in a low baritone voice, "Mr. Stoddard, you have been charged with Felony Arson under Section 28.02 of the Texas Penal Code. Do you understand?"

Jack nodded. "Yes sir."

Judge Bonham looked over at the prosecutor. "Any plea deals we need to get out of the way?"

She grimaced. "No, your honor. Based on the facts, the defendant was offered a deal to plead guilty to a lesser charge, but he declined the offer."

Judge Bonham shifted his focus to Simon. "Mr. Steed, would you care to comment?"

Simon nodded. "Yes, your honor. Based on the facts, the Dallas Police Department failed to give Mr. Stoddard the required Miranda warning. As a result, the prosecutor has no evidence to substantiate a charge of any kind against my client."

Judge Bonham raised an eyebrow. "Ms. Weiss, is that an accurate statement?"

She sighed. "That part is true. The arresting officer did not use the proper wording in the Miranda warning. However, we do have other evidence that will support a charge of Felony Arson."

Simon spoke up right away. "But you have no evidence, circumstantial or direct, tying my client to the scene of the crime."

Judge Bonham glared down at the prosecutor. "Is that correct?"

Janet's face contorted as if she were in pain. "The investigation is ongoing."

Judge Bonham boomed, "My court is not going to allow the Dallas District Attorney's Office to conduct discovery during trial. Since your office brought the charge, you must either have a case or you must dismiss until you do have it."

The prosecutor's lips were pursed. "Yes, your honor. We will dismiss the charge against Mr. Stoddard."

Judge Bonham glanced over at Simon. "Mr. Steed,

I see you're back in action."

Simon cracked a smile. "Yes, I hope to start picking up some court appointed cases again if possible."

"Be here at 8:30 am tomorrow."

"Thank you, judge."

Simon exited the courtroom feeling almost exhilarated. He could not remember the last time he felt this way. He walked to the end of the hallway to where the elevator was located. A sign posted on it indicating it was temporarily out of order for maintenance purposes.

Simon walked down one flight of stairs, when he heard a familiar man's voice. Two men were ascending the stairs and rounded the corner to the landing at the same time as Simon.

One of the men froze in his tracks when he spotted Simon. A grin slowly appeared on his round face. "I can't believe it. Simon Steed, in the flesh."

Simon frowned until he recognized the man as Jon Stowers, a classmate at law school. Jon had not changed much in appearance. He was still a plump man with a receding hairline. His Brooks Brothers suit coat buttons were straining to conceal his protruding stomach. Even as a law student, Jon always wore expensive starched white dress shirts garnished with an Armani silk tie.

Simon had not seen him since the day Jon tumbled down the steps of the law library during graduation and sustained a severe injury. He knew the precise moment when Jon would trip. It did not take much for Jon to provoke Simon because he despised him.

Simon snapped, "I haven't seen you since you took that tumble at graduation."

Jon's face contorted. "Uh, yes... So, Simon, I heard you were doing criminal law defense work. I never envisioned you going into that kind of law."

Simon sneered. "It pays the bills."

In a voice laden with sarcasm, Jon said, "I didn't realize Dallas County was so generous with the taxpayer's money paying court appointed attorneys."

Simon pursed his lips. "What kind of law do you practice?"

His face lit up. "I'm a partner at Hughes and Litze. The largest law firm in Dallas."

Jon gestured toward the other man, who was tall, thin, with thick blond hair, dressed in a charcoal gray suit, white shirt, and red tie. "This is my law clerk, Carter Dillion. He's a third-year student at SMU and in the top ten percent of his class, academically."

The man smiled and said, "Nice to meet you."

Before Simon could respond, Jon said, "Carter, Simon here was rated near the top of our class. While I think you would fit in nicely at our firm, you might consider pursuing a career as a court appointed criminal defense attorney."

Jon barely finished the sentence before he burst out laughing.

Simon felt the veins in his neck bulging from anger. His disdain for Jon had not diminished over the years.

"Good to catch up with you, Simon," Jon said. "However, we're due in court."

Simon stood frozen without saying a word. Jon gave Simon a playful pat on the shoulder as he walked past him.

It took all the willpower Simon could muster to keep from slugging Jon. He turned his head and watched as the two men ascended the stairs and disappeared around the corner.

Simon took several deep breaths to compose himself and ambled down the stairs to the first floor. He kept running through his head the whole exchange of words with Jon.

I was provoked but didn't cause any harm to that bastard!

Chapter 13

Friday afternoon at 4:00 pm, a courier arrived at his office with three boxes from the Law Office of Rowan Stedman and Associates. Simon broke the seal on one of the boxes and peered inside. It was full of individual account statements and other materials arranged in a haphazard manner. He surmised that Rowan had done this on purpose to make his job of reviewing them more difficult.

Simon cleared everything off his desk except for the telephone so he could have room to organize the statements in neat stacks. After an hour, he decided to call it a day and head home. As Simon was about to stand up and leave, his phone rang. He groaned and picked up the receiver.

"Hello, this is Simon Steed."

"Simon, this is Veronica Steele."

"Hello, Veronica, I'm glad you called. I received several boxes from Rowan Stedman an hour ago."

"Good. That's why I was calling, to see if you had gotten them or not."

He leaned back in his chair. "I've only begun going through them. They are completely disorganized so I will come into my office early tomorrow and sort them. Would you be available late Saturday to review them with me at my office?"

"Of course. But would you possibly be able to meet with me at my home?"

His mouth dropped open. "At your home?"

"Yes, Sterling is out of town, and I have engagement in the Park Cities until about 4:00 pm."

"Are you sure that's wise for us to meet there?"

She snickered. "Of course, it's just fine. It would be a big help to me if you would come here."

Simon sighed. "Okay, what time would work for you?"

"You're a dear. 5:00 pm."

"I'll be there. What is your address?"

Veronica cackled. "The address is not visible from the street but it's the only contemporary home on Beverly Drive between Armstrong and Douglas. You can't miss it."

Simon cocked his head. "Okay, I'll find it."

"Thank you, bye."

Before he could respond, the dial tone hummed.

Why does she have to be so mysterious? Am I making a huge mistake going to her house?

Chapter 14

Simon arrived at his office Saturday morning at 8:00 am. He spent the morning reviewing the statements and organizing them by account type and number. Always methodical as well as meticulous, Simon perused every statement to make sure it was for the period the restraining order was in effect, and then highlighted several transactions he thought might be suspicious. He sat straight up in his chair.

What about the Compass account? There's no documentation for it! Was it an oversight or deliberately not included?

* * *

At 3:30 pm, Simon loaded a box of records into the trunk of his car. He was able to pare down the relevant materials from three boxes to one box. Simon pulled out of the Oak Cliff Bank underground parking onto Zang Boulevard. The traffic was light on the freeway Saturday afternoon. He took the Mockingbird exit off the Central Expressway and headed west to the Hillcrest intersection and took a left. Simon arrived

at the intersection of Hillcrest and Beverly Drive at
4:00 pm.

He surmised it was too early to show up at the
Steele residence but thought he would locate the
residence and then go in search of a coffee shop he
frequented in nearby Snider Plaza. The coffee shop
was located right across from the campus where he
attended law school.

Simon took a right on Beverly Drive and drove
his Pontiac up the posh street lined with mansion
after mansion. He soon approached the Douglas
intersection.

Scanning both sides of the street searching for
a contemporary designed house, he slowed down
the car until it crawled down Beverly Drive. All
the houses so far seemed to be variations of Tudor-
influenced architecture.

At last Simon spotted what had to be the Steeles'
house on his left. He parked his car across the street
and studied the layout for a few seconds.

He understood now why Veronica did not give
him the address, because he could not see signage
anywhere. As Simon eased away from the curb, he
noticed a man and Veronica behind a low neatly
trimmed hedge of bushes.

He shifted his car into park and watched. They
appeared to be talking. His torso jolted as he identified the man as Boris Denucci.

*Wait a minute, when I told Veronica that this
character came to my office to discuss her divorce, she*

said she didn't know him! Why is he here?

After a few more minutes, the man got into a car parked in the driveway and Veronica walked onto her front porch and entered her house through the front door. Boris backed his car slowly out of the driveway and drove east on Beverly Drive.

Just as Simon pulled away from the curb, he heard a siren and saw flashing red lights in his rear-view mirror. A Highland Park Police car pulled up right behind him.

Simon rolled down his window and fished his wallet out of his pocket. A police officer exited his squad car and slowly strolled up to the driver's side of Simon's car. He leaned over and his eyes carefully swept the interior of the Pontiac.

"I'm Officer Daniels. May I see your driver's license?"

Simon handed him his license.

The man studied it a few seconds. "It appears, Mr. Steed, that you don't live around here, judging by the 75224 zip code."

Simon nodded. "Yes, I live in Oak Cliff."

Officer Daniels frowned. "What brings you to Highland Park?"

Simon pointed in the direction of the Steeles' residence. "I have a business meeting there at 5:00 pm."

The police officer narrowed his eyes. "That's over an hour away. Why are you here this early parked across the street?"

"Because I wanted to know where the Steeles

lived so I wouldn't be late. I intended to go to grab a coffee in Snider Plaza before going there."

Officer Daniels sighed. "What kind of business meeting are you having with the Steeles?"

"I'm an attorney. I'm meeting with Mrs. Steele on a legal matter."

He growled. "Show me your State of Texas Bar Card."

Simon fished it out of his wallet and handed it to the police officer.

"I'll be right back," he said.

Simon watched in his rearview mirror as Officer Daniels slid into the driver's seat of his squad car. He surmised that the police officer was checking to see if he had any outstanding warrants.

After a few minutes, Officer Daniels ambled back up to the Pontiac and handed him his license and bar card. "Mr. Steed, you're free to go."

Simon looked at him. "Officer Daniels, may I ask why you pulled me over?"

The police officer chuckled. "People in this type of neighborhood call the police anytime they see something suspicious. You parked here in a 1960s Pontiac made some folks wonder what you were up to."

Simon grimaced. "I see. Thank you, officer."

* * *

A few minutes before 5:00 pm, Simon drove the short distance from Snider Plaza back over to Beverly

Drive. He wondered if Officer Daniels was still in the vicinity. He pulled his car into the Steeles' driveway and parked in the location where Boris Denucci had parked earlier in the day.

The Steele residence was a two-story, sleek contemporary-designed home with a mixture of beautiful wood interwoven with stone. The landscaping was freshly manicured, a perfect fit for the styling of the home.

Simon bounded up to the front porch with a box of account statements. He managed to ring the doorbell without setting down the box. After a couple of minutes, the front door swung open.

Veronica Steele stood in the open doorway smiling. Her brunette hair was neatly coifed, and her blue eyes dazzled in the sunlight. She was dressed in a white blouse, faded but expensive blue jeans, and brown flats.

"Hello, Simon, right on time as always. Please come in." She stepped aside as he entered the residence.

The sunlight filtered in through floor to ceiling windows at the rear of the house overlooking an infinity edged swimming pool.

"Let's go to my work area." Veronica turned around and headed toward the back of the house.

Simon followed her. Large abstract pieces of art adorned the museum-quality white walls. The rooms were furnished with B&B Italia furniture, with a couple of Eames chairs thrown in for good measure.

Simon said, "You have a beautiful home."

Veronica spun around and flashed a smile. "Thank you, Simon."

She led him to a large room in the left rear part of the house. Various pictures of her from her modeling days decorated one entire wall. A treadmill and weight workout station were situated in one corner and a desk, table, two chairs, and a loveseat filled the remainder of the room.

Veronica said, "Just set the box down on the table." She arranged the two chairs, so they were sitting side by side. "Simon, would you care for a glass of wine?"

His eyes widened. "Sure, if you're having one."

She winked at him. "I wouldn't want you to drink alone."

Veronica returned with two empty wine glasses and a bottle of Flowers Chardonnay. "I brought the bottle because I thought we might want a second glass."

She poured two glasses of wine while Simon spread the account papers across the table. Veronica handed him a full glass of wine.

"Thank you. I have marked all the transactions which I want you to review. See if anything looks suspicious to you."

She leaned in to get a closer look and went through each statement. "This all looks normal to me."

Simon took a swig of wine. "Do you see any account that's missing?"

Veronica cocked her head. "Not that I'm aware

of... Wait a minute, there's no Compass statements."

He nodded. "Precisely. No Compass statements were included in any of the materials I received. What I don't know if that was intentional or just an oversight on their part."

Her face contorted. "I hate that man. I just wish he would vanish from the earth."

Simon took another drink of wine. "I can promise you I will bring it up at the hearing."

Veronica threw up her hands as she sobbed. "Simon, I wished I possessed those powers you have. I wouldn't hesitate to kill him."

He patted her shoulder. "I will do everything I can to get you a huge chunk of the estate."

At once, she stopped weeping and her eyes fixated on him. "I wish the hell that he would provoke you."

Simon pursed his lips.

"Maybe he will."

Expressionless, he stared at her.

Chapter 15

On Monday, Simon arrived at the Family District Court fifteen minutes before the scheduled 10:00 am hearing in the Steele divorce. He wondered if Veronica or her husband were going to appear for the hearing. Neither the plaintiff nor respondent are required to appear at preliminary hearings of this nature.

As Simon entered the courtroom, he spotted Rowan Stedman and a man he presumed to be Sterling Steele seated at one of the counsel tables. He nodded at Rowan as he took a seat at the other table.

Simon marveled at the difference in atmosphere between Family District Court and a District Court in a criminal case. In the context of a criminal case, there was always an abundance of activity with attorneys scurrying around making plea deals and filing motions. The Family District Court today was calm in comparison.

Two attorneys stood below the bench of the presiding judge, Wilford Dameron. They appeared to conclude their business and exited the courtroom.

A few minutes later, Judge Dameron looked down at them and motioned Rowan and Simon to approach the bench. "It appears, Mr. Stedman, you have filed a motion challenging the restraining order on Mr. Steele's financial accounts?" He leaned forward just enough to look over the top of his glasses. Judge Dameron said, "What evidence do you have to overturn the order?"

Rowan glanced over his shoulder. "I would like to put Mr. Steele on the stand to provide such evidence."

Judge Dameron said, "Very well. Take your seats."

Sterling Steele took the stand and was sworn in by Judge Dameron.

Sterling was a tall man with chiseled features and thick dark hair graying a bit at the temples. He was impeccably dressed in a charcoal gray designer suit, white shirt and red tie. Simon thought that Sterling could have easily been a model like his wife in his younger years.

Rowan said, "Mr. Steele, could you please state your name for the record?"

In a deep booming voice, Sterling said, "Sterling Hayward Steele."

"What do you do for a living, Mr. Steele?"

Sterling looked over at Simon for the first time. "I'm an investment adviser."

Rowan cocked his head. "Can you explain what exactly an investment adviser does on a daily basis?"

"It varies from advisor to advisor. I not only advise

but also invest myself. What better way to convince clients to trust your advice than to show them how to successfully invest."

Rowan glanced over at Simon. "Did plaintiff's counsel have you served with a subpoena duces tecum requesting a list of all your financial accounts and statements for all activity since the effective date of the restraining order?"

Sterling nodded. "Yes."

"And did you provide the requested documents?"

"Of course! They were couriered to his office in Oak Cliff." Sterling rolled eyes.

Simon surmised that having his wife represented by an attorney in Oak Cliff was insulting to him, even as a respondent in a divorce matter.

Rowan leaned forward. "Are any of these accounts that are listed individually in your name used for business purposes?"

Sterling smirked. "All but the checking and saving accounts at NorthPark Bank and the Republic Bank of Dallas are business accounts."

"Is it fair to say then that your day-to-day personal expenses would come from one these accounts?"

Sterling boomed, "Absolutely!"

Rowan bounced in his chair. "Would it also be fair to say that an order restraining the other accounts should beyond the scope of any restraining order, since it is part of your livelihood?"

"That's correct."

Rowan looked up at Judge Dameron. "I pass the witness."

Simon glanced down at his legal pad. "Mr. Steele, you have testified that you provided a list of all your financial accounts and statements for all the activities since the effective date of the restraining order, correct?"

Sterling frowned. "You heard me, didn't you?"

Judge Dameron looked down at Sterling. "Mr. Steele, just answer the question."

Sterling barked, "Yes."

Simon stood up. "Your honor, I have provided a complete list of all the accounts provided by Mr. Steele. I would like to have him review it to make sure it contains all his accounts."

Judge Dameron looked over at Rowan. "Any objection, Mr. Stedman?"

Rowan's face wore what Simon speculated was a sarcastic smirk.

"No, your honor," he said, "that's fine."

Simon walked up to the witness stand and handed the paper to Sterling. "Please carefully review the list to make sure it is one hundred percent accurate."

Sterling sighed and spent a few minutes studying the list. He looked up. "It's complete."

Simon said, "May I have the list back?"

Sterling shoved it into his hand, and Simon returned to the counsel table and plopped down in his chair. "Mr. Steele, this list isn't complete, is it?"

Sterling narrowed his eyes. "I said it was complete and it is."

Simon fished into his briefcase and pulled out a

Compass Bank deposit slip. "The list does not contain this Compass Bank account, does it?"

Through gritted teeth, Rowan said, "Let me see that."

Simon handed Rowan the deposit slip. He perused it.

Judge Dameron said, "Please pass me the deposit slip."

Rowan ambled up to the bench and handed the paper to the judge. He studied it for a few seconds before glaring down at Sterling. "Mr. Steele, your name is on this account. Is this your account?"

Sterling's face turned crimson from anger and embarrassment. "Yes, it's my damn account."

"Motion to remove the restraining order is hereby denied," Judge Dameron bellowed. "The restraining order will remain in effect until the divorce is finalized."

Simon cracked a slight smile as he sat and watched Sterling climb down off the witness stand. He took his time putting his legal pad into his brief-case and then waited for Sterling and Rowan to exit the courtroom before leaving.

As soon as he came outside the courtroom, Sterling confronted him. The veins in his neck were bulging. He had a three-inch height advantage and peered down at Simon. "How the hell did you know about that account. Did Veronica find out?"

Simon took a deep breath to remain calm. "That's attorney client privilege."

Sterling grabbed Simon by his suit coat lapels. "You sorry bastard."

Simon's anger boiled inside but he remained still. Both of them resembled boxers trying to stare each other down prior to a championship fight. Rowan stepped up and grabbed both men by the arm. "Sterling, this isn't the time or place for this. Back away, and let's go."

A crowd of onlookers had formed, watching the spectacle between the men. Sterling jerked his hands away from Simon's lapels. "This isn't over."

Rowan said, "Come on, Sterling. Let's get the hell out of here."

Simon froze and watched the two men walk away.

Sterling, if this had happened in the past, you would soon encounter your demise.

* * *

Simon worked later than usual and decided to stop for some barbecue at Red Bryan's Smokehouse on Jefferson Boulevard before heading home to Wynnewood North. He pulled into his driveway at 7:50 pm. It was an overcast dark night. Simon grabbed his briefcase off the front passenger seat and exited the Pontiac. He shot a glance over at his neighbor's windows, but no lights were on.

All of a sudden, Simon felt the impact and a sharp pain in the back of his skull, causing him to stumble and crash onto the driveway. Out of the side of his left eye, he could see a dark figure of a man hovering over him. The man was dressed in black and wearing a ski mask.

Simon lay still, hoping the man would think he was unconscious. He surmised that if he did not resist, then maybe the assailant would just rob him of his valuables and leave.

A gloved hand raised Simon's right hand off the ground and forced it around something with a solid surface. Simon waited for the man to start fishing through his pockets, but nothing happened. Then footsteps ran away from him down the driveway toward the street.

Simon remained motionless, trying to process what just happened, when a car's engine started up and its tires squealed as it sped away down the street. He sat up and grabbed the back of his head and felt a bump underneath his hair. Simon reached for the rear bumper of his Pontiac and used it as support to stand up. By instinct, he felt for his wallet inside his suitcoat jacket. He sighed in relief to find it still there. Simon snatched his briefcase off the driveway and trudged slowly across his lawn to his front door.

Why did someone just assault me for no apparent reason?

He was fumbling with his keys, trying to unlock the front door when the sounds of footsteps behind him made him freeze. Then Simon's body jolted as he spun around to face the direction of where he heard the footsteps.

A woman's voice said, "Simon, are you all right?"

"Raven?"

She seized his arm. "What happened? I heard a noise and looked out my bedroom window. All that I could see in the darkness was a body lying in your driveway."

Simon rubbed the back of his head. "Somebody hit me in the head from behind."

Raven took the keys from his hand and unlocked the door. "Let's get you inside."

She led him over to the sofa and he sat down. "Bend your head down so I can have a look."

He ducked his head and felt her fingers rub his scalp.

Raven said, "There doesn't seem to be any open wound. So, you're lucky there. Would you like me to get some ice to put on it?"

Simon shook his head. "No, that's fine, thank you."

She glanced over at his console. "Well, how about I put an album on for you."

He leaned back on the sofa. "That would be nice."

Raven squatted down at the console and started flipping through his albums. "What are you in the mood to hear?"

He looked over at her. "Surprise me."

"As I recall when I first met you, you were listening to the Rolling Stones. Well, how about a little Beatles to round out your 1960s taste?"

Simon managed a slight smile. "That sounds

wonderful." He watched as she took care when removing a disc from the Beatles' White Album.

The disc hissed and cracked as the needle dragged on the vinyl surface. The familiar guitar riffs from "Revolution 1." reverberated from the speakers.

Raven spun around. "I've always loved this song."

He watched as she danced over to where he sat and plopped down near him on the sofa.

Simon said, "Do you always start your albums on Side 2., or in this case, Side 4. since it's a double album?"

Raven smiled. "I haven't had a record player since I was a little girl, but yes. The same is true when I went to the movies. My family was never on time to see the beginning of movies. So, we would watch the end and then the beginning up until where we started."

He remembered that was the same as his childhood. His dad worked long hours and by the time the family sat down to dinner, it was already well into the night. They often arrived at the theater an hour after the movie started. Simon had not thought about that experience for an exceptionally long time.

Raven's face hardened. "Why do you think someone assaulted you?"

He shrugged. "I don't have any idea. I assumed he was going to rob me, but he didn't take my wallet or briefcase. Maybe something spooked him. But you know what was strange about the whole occurrence."

She cocked her head. "What was that?"

Simon extended his right hand. "I distinctly remember feeling a gloved hand lift my right hand and squeeze it around some hard object."

"That's very strange. Why would he do that?"

He smirked. "I don't have the slightest clue. I was lying very still, and I think the assailant thought I was unconscious. But that still doesn't explain the whole hand business."

Simon and Raven talked until the needle skipped in the dead zone at the end of the disc. She glanced down at her watch. "It's getting late, and I better get going. Would you like me to flip the album over or put it up before I go?"

He groaned as he managed to stand up. "Just flip it over and I'll listen to the other side tomorrow."

He watched Raven lift the album by the edges and flip it over to Side 3. She closed the lid of the console with a gentle touch.

"There. It will be waiting for you tomorrow."

He chuckled. "Thank you."

Raven smiled. "You're very welcome. Get some rest."

He gestured toward the den. "I'm going to watch a little television and then hit the sack."

She patted his arm as she walked by and opened the front door.

Simon said, "Thank you for coming over to check on me tonight."

Without turning around, she said, "Of course" and scooted down the steps to the sidewalk.

He locked the front door and ambled into his

kitchen over to the refrigerator. Simon swung open the door and pulled out a can of Coors Light. Before popping it open, he nestled the cold can on the bump on the back of his head. The coolness of the can helped the throbbing subside.

Simon retreated to his den and plopped down on the overstuffed chair facing the television and took a huge swig of beer. He leaned back into the chair and closed his eyes.

Why did someone jump me in my driveway? I wonder if Sterling Steele sent Boris Denucci to rough me up. That character made thinly veiled threats about coming back to Oak Cliff and banished his pistol.

But I saw Denucci at the Steeles' residence talking to Veronica. That doesn't make sense!

Simon rose from the chair and switched on his television set. He flipped through the four channels available and decided to watch an old re-run of the 1950s sitcom Our Miss Brooks on Channel 11. He sank back into the overstuffed chair and caught himself dosing off. He turned the television set off and walked over to the windows.

Although Simon hesitated before peering through the venetian blinds at Raven's house, he could not resist and cracked open the blinds. The light in her bedroom was illuminated. Her silhouetted figure was hovering near the window and appeared to be talking on the telephone.

Who is she talking to at this time of night?

Chapter 16

Tuesday afternoon, Simon had just finished preparing a motion to file in the morning at the courthouse. As he leaned back in his chair, the phone rang. Simon glanced at his wristwatch. It was 5:15 pm.

He grabbed the receiver. "Hello, this is Simon Steed."

"Hello Simon," a woman's voice said, "this is Veronica."

He picked a pen off his desk. "Hello, Veronica, how are things?"

He thought he heard a sigh. "Sterling is becoming more intolerable. He was furious about you bringing up the Compass account in court. He wanted to know how you found out about it. I lied and told him I had no idea."

"I'm so sorry. He was very angry with me after the court hearing. He grabbed my coat lapels. I thought he was going to hit me."

"That's horrific. Listen, Simon, I would really like to talk to you tonight."

Simon frowned. "Well, I guess I can wait in my office for you."

He thought he heard her sniffle and suspected she might be crying.

"May I come to your house tonight?"

His mouth dropped open. "Ah-h-h, I suppose so."

"Oh, thank you!"

He rested his right elbow on the desk. "Let me give you the address. It's—"

"I already have your address. I looked you up in the phone book."

"Oh, okay. Would 7:00 pm work for you?"

"Perfect. See you then."

The dial tone hummed before he could say goodbye. He scratched his head.

This case is getting crazier by the minute!

* * *

Simon downed a frozen dinner and cleaned up. It was 6:45 pm. He pondered why Veronica wanted to come to his house and if she would be on time. Simon decided to listen to an album in the living room while he waited.

As he was about to switch on the console, a gap in the curtains revealed the headlights of a car as it pulled into his driveway. From the light over his front porch, Simon caught sight of a sleek white sports car.

He backed away from the window and stood next to the front door. A few minutes later, the doorbell rang. Simon peered out of the peep hole. Veronica stared straight at the peep hole, as if she could see him.

He swung open the door. "Good evening, Veronica."

She was dressed in faded blue jeans, a black shirt, a black leather tailored jacket, and matching handbag. Her hair was pulled back in a ponytail. She seemed to force a smile. "Hi Simon, may I come in?"

He stood to the side. "Of course."

She walked inside with her head rotating back and forth as she surveyed the living room.

Simon locked the door behind her. "Did you have any trouble finding my house?"

Veronica shook her head. "No, I'm pretty good with a map. I've never been over here before."

"You mean my neighborhood, Wynnewood North?"

"Yes. The only time I've been to Oak Cliff was to go to your office."

He gestured with his right hand toward the sofa. "Please have a seat."

She wiped the sofa with her hand before she perched on the end, making as little contact as possible with the surface. Simon surmised she was uncomfortable outside the bubble of the Park Cities. He plopped down into the overstuffed chair next to the sofa.

"You have interesting décor," Veronica said.

Simon smiled. "I suppose so. It's similar to the furniture I had growing up. In fact, I spent the first part of my childhood in this house."

She cocked her head. "Did you inherit the house?"

He shook his head. "No, I purchased it just last year."

"Really?"

"May I get you a glass of wine or anything to drink?"

Veronica shook her head. "No, I'm fine. Thank you."

Simon leaned forward. "So, what did you want to discuss?"

Her lips pursed. "We need to do something about Sterling. I can't wait until the divorce is finalized."

Scowling, he squinted. "Do you mean something like filing for a restraining order to keep him away from you."

She fished in her handbag, pulled out a tissue, and dabbed the corners of her eyes. "No, something more drastic."

His eyes widened. "What exactly do you have in mind?"

"You saw for yourself what he's capable of doing." Her face contorted. "Didn't you say he grabbed you by your coat lapels?"

Simon nodded. "Yes, he certainly created a scene outside the courtroom. I thought for sure he was going to hit me, and he probably would have if Rowan hadn't intervened."

She bounced on the sofa. "How did that make you feel?"

He exhaled a deep breath. "Very angry. I could feel my veins bulging in my neck."

Veronica was laser focused on him. "Did he provoke you like those occurrences you told me about in the past? Could you have mentally caused him harm?"

Simon shifted in the chair. "I thought about that as I watched him and Rowan walk away from me down the hall. In the past, I would have caused some catastrophic to happen to him."

She twisted on the sofa. "Why didn't you, Simon? It would have solved our problems."

His lips tightened. "Our problems?"

She nodded with increased vigor. "Yes, damn it, our problems. Didn't you say Sterling sent some character to threaten you in your office? You said the guy even showed you his pistol."

Simon groaned. "Yes, Boris Denucci. He said he would be coming back to Oak Cliff. That was less than a subtle threat."

"And did he?"

He sighed. "I think so. My next door neighbor saw some guy who fits his description hanging around my house one evening when I wasn't home."

Veronica scooted down to the end of the sofa until she was sitting next to his chair. "Don't you under-stand that he isn't ever going to stop until you're intimidated and drop the divorce, or you're dead?"

Simon leaned back and took a deep breath. "That may be true. I haven't told you this, but someone assaulted me last night in my driveway."

Her mouth dropped open. "What happened?"

He reached up and touched the back of his head. "I felt the sudden sharp pain in the back of my head and lost my balance. I crumpled down on my driveway and lay still. Although I was in a fog, I wanted the assailant to think I was unconscious. I thought I was just being robbed and the assailant would probably grab my wallet and leave me alone."

She reached over and touched his knee. "What happened then?"

He cocked his head. "It was strange. A gloved hand picked up my right hand and squeezed it around some hard object. After that, I heard footsteps run away down my driveway. Then a car started up and the tires squealed as he drove away. When I managed to sit up, I discovered my wallet was still in my coat pocket and my briefcase was untouched, lying near me on the driveway."

Veronica appeared to be hanging on to his every word. "That's weird. Did you call the police?"

Simon shook his head. "No, my neighbor heard something and looked out her window. She didn't see the assailant but noticed my body lying on the driveway. She rushed over and helped me get inside my house." He chuckled and pointed at his console. "It's kind of funny. I get assaulted in my driveway one minute and the next minute I'm listening to a record album with my neighbor."

She leaned over and grabbed his arm. "Simon, you have got to use your powers to do something about Sterling."

Simon looked deep into her eyes. "I can, but I won't. I'm not ever going back to that dark place in my life."

Veronica released his arm and growled, "The only reason I hired you as my attorney was to take advantage of your powers. Since you're of no use to me, you're fired as my attorney! But you can't avoid your entanglement with me."

He narrowed his eyes. "What do you mean?"

She sneered and stood up. "You'll find out soon enough"

He stood up and followed her to the front door. Veronica paused a few feet short of it and walked over to his console and opened the lid. Simon froze in his tracks and was laser focused on her. She stared down at Side 3. of the Beatles' White Album that Raven had set up last night for him to hear this evening.

Veronica gazed up at him. Her face was pale white and distorted. She bellowed, "Who told you?"

He recoiled. "Who told me what?"

Trembling, Veronica gritted her teeth and lunged toward him. "You were going to play that song and taunt me, weren't you?"

He backed up and shrugged. "I'm sorry, but I don't know what you're talking about."

She hissed, "You're lying, you bastard. It was Sterling, wasn't it? He told you one of my personalities is Sexy Sadie, didn't he?"

Simon cocked his head. "No one told me anything about that."

Veronica stared at him for a few seconds before storming over to the front door. She unlocked it as if breaking a twig from a tree trunk and stomped outside. He watched from the front porch as she backed out of his driveway and sped off down his street into darkness.

Sexy Sadie? Wait a minute, I do remember Rowan Stedman asking me if I had met Sadie yet!

Simon's stomach twisted into knots. He ambled over to his console and dropped the needle of the stereo onto the song, *Sexy Sadie*. The needle scratched a second before the piano introduction followed by John Lennon singing:

Sexy Sadie what have you done?
You made a fool of everyone

Simon jumped when his doorbell rang. He reached down and scratched the surface of the record as he picked the needle up off the album.

Did Veronica come back? She'll go ballistic if she heard me playing that song!

Simon crept over to the front door and peered out through the peephole. He released a heavy sigh and then opened the door. Steve Paxton, his neighbor from across the street, stood with his hands in his pockets on his porch.

Simon said, "Steve?"

"Hi, Simon, I hope I'm not interrupting anything."

Simon said, "No, not at all. Would you like to come inside?"

He shook his head. "No, I just dropped by to invite you to our house tomorrow night. Since the weather is so nice for January, we thought we'd invite the neighbors over for a post-holiday celebration of sorts in our front yard. It will give all of us a chance to meet our neighbors and an excuse for me to turn on the Christmas lights one last time."

"That's very nice of you to ask me. What time is the event?"

Steve grinned. "From 7:00 pm until 10:00 pm. I hope you can make it."

Simon smiled. "I will certainly try. I haven't met many of the neighbors since I've been here."

Steve pointed over at Simon's driveway. "By the way, I happened to see that sleek Jaguar XJ6 parked in your driveway earlier. I don't suppose you got a new car."

Simon shook his head. "No, that belongs to an unusual, and now former, client of mine."

Steve wrinkled his forehead. "Why is she unusual?"

Simon sighed. "She wanted to come to my house tonight to talk. Until she fired me tonight, I represented her in her divorce case. I can't get into any specifics as to what we talked about, but she was upset with me because I wouldn't do something for her. As she was about to leave, for some reason she walked over to my console. When she saw what was on my turntable, she turned white as a sheet and seemed to snap. To be honest, I feared what she might do next."

Steve's eyes lit up. "What on your turntable triggered that kind of reaction?"

"Are you familiar with the Beatles' *White Album*?"

He nodded. "Of course, everyone is."

Simon glanced over at his console. "Remember the song, Sexy Sadie?"

"Sure. Sexy Sadie, what have you done?"

Simon nodded. "Precisely. This woman said Sexy Sadie was one of her personalities and wondered how I knew that."

Steve rubbed his head. "I see now why you said she was unusual. She sounds crazy to me. At least she has good taste in cars." He snickered at his own comment.

Simon said, "She definitely has expensive tastes."

Steve stepped down from the porch. "I've got to go invite some more neighbors before it gets too late. I'll see you tomorrow, Simon."

Simon waved, closed, and locked the door. He entered his den and thought about turning on the television but instead ambled over to the windows. He cracked open the venetian blinds and peeked at his next door neighbor's house.

None of the interior lights was illuminated.

I hope Raven comes to the neighborhood event tomorrow night. Why haven't I seen her lately?

Chapter 17

Wednesday morning, Simon was able to pick up two more court-appointed cases. His case load almost matched the load he had maintained prior to being hospitalized at Parkland Behavior Health Center. He spent the afternoon drafting several motions to file later that week.

At 5:00 pm, Simon decided to call it day. The more he thought about the neighborhood event that evening, the more excited he felt to attend it. In the past, he would have avoided any kind of social event, not that he received many invitations.

The temperature all day had hovered around the upper sixties. The sky was clear outside, which made it a perfect setting for his neighborhood event. Simon pulled into his driveway at 5:20 pm. The Paxtons' house was lit up and folding chairs already dotted the lawn.

* * *

Promptly at 7:00 pm, Simon peered out of the crack in the living room drapes at the Paxton's house. Several people milled around in the front yard. He decided he would make his appearance at 7:15 pm.

Before leaving, Simon made his way back to the den. He had hoped to catch a glimpse of Raven's silhouette in her bedroom window.

Much to his disappointment, no light was on in the house. Simon grabbed a light jacket before exiting his house. He took his time trudging down his sidewalk and crossed the street.

Steve Paxton waved him over to where he stood next to a tall lean man. "Simon, thank you for coming," Steve said. "As you can see, Simon lives across the street."

He pointed to his left. "This is Sam Zimmerman. Sam lives at the end of the street."

Simon and Sam shook hands.

Sam said, "Simon, how long have you lived here?"

Simon glanced over at his house. "About a year, this go-round. I grew up in this house as a kid."

Sam eyes lit up. "Really? That's interesting you came back home after all these years."

Simon tugged at his ear. "I happened to see it for sale one day in the *Dallas Morning News* and made an offer on it the next day."

"Well, welcome home," Sam said. "Have you had a chance to meet many neighbors?"

Simon shook his head. "No, only Steve here, a man named Ted Clements, who lives on the street behind me and my next door neighbor, Raven." He gestured with his head in the direction of his next door neighbor's house.

Sam shook his head and shrugged. "I don't believe I know any one of those folks. In fact, I thought the house next to yours was vacant." He paused. "Steve will know for sure though," he said with a chuckle. "He keeps up with all the news on this street."

Steve was chatting with a woman but turned around when he heard his name. "Were you talking about me again, Sam?"

Sam nodded. "Yes, Simon says he has met the neighbor who lives next door to him."

Simon pointed at Raven's house. "That house. Her name is Raven Nevers. Did you by chance invite her?"

Steve raised an eyebrow. "That house is vacant. But hopefully it won't be for long. I happened to be in my front yard when I met a real estate agent from Ebby Halliday. He stopped by to put a lock box on the front door."

Simon felt a chill shoot down his spine. "Are you sure?"

Steve said, "Go over and check it out. You'll see the box."

Simon felt clammy. "I... I guess maybe I was confused. Perhaps she lives farther down the block."

Steve gave him a playful slap on the shoulder. "You look like you could use an adult beverage."

Simon rubbed his brow. "I think I do."

"That tub is full of beer and wine." Steve pointed over to a table near the front door. "Go help yourself."

"Thank you." Simon let out a brief sigh of relief

to have a moment to himself. He ambled over to the table and fished out a can of Bud Light."

A woman's voice to his left said, "Do you live in the house directly across from the Paxtons?"

He glanced over at where he heard the voice. A stout mid-sixties woman with gray hair stood smiling at him.

"Uh, yes, I live there."

The woman extended her hand. "I'm Wanda Silks. I live three doors down from you."

Simon shook her hand. "It's nice to meet you, Wanda. I'm Simon Steed."

"You haven't lived there long, have you?" Wanda said.

He took a swig of beer. "I have been here around a year."

She said, "My husband Dan and I moved here fifteen years ago."

"That's a long time. You must know just about everyone in the neighborhood."

Wanda smiled. "I try to get to know my neighbors."

He pointed at the house next door to his house. "Do you know if anyone lives there?"

She pursed her lips. "It's been vacant quite a while. I think it was tied up in a probate matter. A man used to live there but he passed away, I guess just about the time you moved in."

Simon took another swig of beer. "Have you by chance met a woman named Raven Nevers?"

Wanda shrugged. "No, I can't say I have. Why do you ask?"

He grimaced. "I met her not too long ago and thought she lived in the neighborhood."

She raised an eyebrow. "If she does, that's news to me."

Simon sighed. "What about a man named Ted Clements. He and his dog came by my house one night. You can hear his dog barking sometimes at night."

Wanda shook her head. "No, I haven't met him, and I've never heard any dog barking at night." She paused as she patted his arm. "It was nice to meet you, Simon. I've got to go rescue those ladies from my husband. He will talk their ears off, if I don't."

Simon did not respond. He glanced at his watch. It was 8:05 pm.

I've had enough of this!

After tossing his empty beer can in a trash container, Simon walked back to his house. Once he was inside, he made a beeline to the windows in the den. He peaked through the venetian blinds at his next door neighbor's house. No lights were on inside the house.

Simon rushed into his bathroom and opened the medicine cabinet above the sink. He poured the contents of two medications that he was prescribed for his mental illness on the bathroom countertop. One by one, Simon counted out the tablets and was satisfied that he had not forgotten to take them.

Has Monica returned?

* * *

Simon was able to get to sleep at last when he was jolted awake by his doorbell, which seemed to be ringing nonstop. Next came a insistent knocking at his front door.

Simon slipped on some jeans and a T-shirt and sprinted up the hallway to his living room. The knocking got louder as he drew near his front door.

Simon shouted, "Who's there?"

A man's bass voice shouted, "Dallas and Highland Park Police. Open the door."

He switched on the porch light and peered through the peephole in the door. A uniformed police officer and a tall man dressed in a dark suit stood on his front porch, staring at the door.

Simon cracked the front door open. "What's this all about?"

The uniform officer said, "I'm Officer Stapleton, Dallas Police Department, and this is Detective Williams, Highland Park Police Department. May we come inside?"

Simon's eyes widened. "Of course, please come in."

The two men came inside. Detective Williams pulled his badge out of his pocket and showed it to Simon. "Are you Simon Steed?"

Simon nodded. "Yes, I am."

Detective Williams said, "Where were you between 7:00 pm and 8:00 pm tonight?"

Simon pointed toward the front of his house. "I was across the street in the front yard. My neighbors were having a neighborhood party."

"What your neighbors' names?"

"Steve and Mary Paxton."

Officer Stapleton said, "You want me to go check it out?"

Detective Williams nodded. "Yes, officer, thank you."

"How many people attended this event?"

Simon glanced up at the ceiling as if this would help him remember. "Fifteen or maybe twenty."

The Detective jotted on a small notepad. "Who did you talk to during your time there?"

"Steve, my neighbor, Sam Zimmerman who lives at the end of the street, and a woman named Wanda Silks. She lives a few doors down from me."

"When exactly did you arrive at this event?"

Simon scratched his head. "7:15 and I left a little after 8:00 pm. Detective, can you tell what this is all about?"

Detective Williams looked up from jotting on his pad. "Are you familiar with Veronica Steele?"

Simon's eyes widened. "Yes, she used to be a client of mine. I'm an attorney and represented her in a divorce matter. Why do you ask?"

"Did she get a divorce?"

He shook his head. "No, the proceeding is still ongoing. But she got angry with me and fired me last night."

Detective Williams furrowed his brows. "What did you do to make her angry?"

Simon took a deep breath and paused before responding. He did not want to go into his telepathic abilities to cause harm to others when he is provoked.

"I'm not certain. She despised her husband. I think she was dissatisfied when I could not speed up the whole divorce process."

Detective Williams rubbed his chin. "Could it be that she fired you because you made a pass at her last night?"

Simon narrowed his eyes. "No, absolutely not. I would never do that with a client."

The detective raised an eyebrow. "She was here last night though, correct?"

He nodded. "Yes, she called me around 5:00 pm at my office and said she wanted to talk to me in person. I offered to remain at my office and meet her there, but she insisted on coming to my house."

Detective Williams scribbled on his pad. "Do you often invite clients over to your house?"

Anger boiled inside Simon, as his stomach churned. "No, never."

"Mrs. Steele said it was you who insisted on meeting her at your house. She indicated you wanted to update her on a recent hearing in her case and you preferred to tell her face to face."

Simon shook his head several times. "That's not true. Her purpose for coming to my house was to try and convince me to help kill her husband. When I refused, she went ballistic. The woman has multiple personalities. She suffers from a mental illness called Dissociative Identity Disorder."

Detective Williams sneered but continued writing on his pad. "And how exactly do you know about her mental condition?"

Simon sighed. "Because she told me. I suffer from the same kind of illness. In fact, that's the reason she told me she wanted me to represent her in the divorce. She believed I could identify with her mental illness. I'm a criminal defense attorney, so I thought it was unusual for her to contact me about representation in a divorce matter."

Detective Williams cocked his head. "That seems a little farfetched. How the hell did she know you had this condition in the first place?"

Simon pursed his lips. "Because her sister was one of my nurses at Parkland Behavioral Health Center. She told Veronica Steele about my illness."

Detective Williams smirked. "The Steeles live in Highland Park. There's no telling how much money they have. Mrs. Steele could hire any high-priced divorce attorney in America. Why in the world would she hire a criminal defense attorney to represent her in something as important as a divorce?"

Simon closed his eyes and took several deep breaths. "Because, detective, I think I possess certain powers. When someone makes me extremely angry, I can wreak havoc upon them telepathically. Veronica Steele wanted me to unleash my powers on her husband, but I refused."

Detective Williams hung on every word. "I don't know whether you're crazy or not. But I do want to determine if you shot and killed Sterling Steele this evening."

A chill shot down Simon's spine and he trembled. "That's horrific! No, I've been here all evening. I told you that."

"Officer Stapleton is checking out your alibi. But Mrs. Steele says she spotted your car in their driveway at 6:45 pm when she was returning from shopping."

Simon was now shaking harder. "That's impossible!"

Detective Williams cracked an incredulous smile. "Do you drive a 1966 Pontiac Lemans, Texas license plate number SNK 773?"

He nodded. "Of course, it's parked in my driveway."

"Well, Mr. Steed, that's the description of the car Mrs. Steele claimed was parked in their driveway. She said you were so infatuated with her that you threatened to kill her husband. Mrs. Steele thought if she showed up while you were there, it would 'pour gasoline on the fire', so to speak. She drove around the neighborhood for about thirty minutes. When she returned home, your car was gone so she went inside and found her husband lying in a pool of blood in the kitchen. She immediately dialed 911. Her neighbor heard a single gunshot earlier around 7:30 pm."

Mouth gaping, Simon stared at the detective. "I don't believe this is happening!"

After a quick knock at the front door, Officer Stapleton stuck his head inside. "Detective, may I have a word with you?"

The two men walked out on Simon's front porch and closed the door behind them. Simon stumbled over to the sofa and plopped down. He took several deep breaths, trying to compose himself.

A few minutes later, the two opened the door and entered the living room. Detective Williams said, "Steve Paxton and Sam Zimmerman corroborate your story."

Simon sighed. "Thank God."

Detective Williams said, "You don't have any trips planned outside of Dallas County, do you?"

Simon shook his head. "No, I've no travel plans."

The detective stuck his pad of paper inside his coat pocket. "While you're not a suspect at the moment, you will remain a person of interest until the investigation is concluded."

Simon locked the door behind them.

I can't believe that bitch is blaming me for the death of her husband!

He headed down the hall toward his bedroom, but reversed course and walked to the other side of his house to the den. In the darkness, he went over to the window and cracked open the venetian blinds.

His mouth dropped open when he spotted the silhouette of a female figure standing near her bedroom window. The figure appeared to be looking out the window at his house.

Am I imagining seeing Raven's silhouette? Hell, I may have even imagined the police came here tonight about Sterling Steele's murder. He whirled around. *For all I know, he may be at home in Highland Park watching a movie on television!*

Simon jumped at the sound of his doorbell ringing. "What now?"

He raced through his house to the living room and peaked through the peephole. Steve Paxton stood on the front porch.

Simon swung open the door. "Hi Steve, is everything okay?"

He nodded. "Yes, but I'm not use to be questioned by the police, especially this late at night."

Simon grimaced. "Listen, I'm so sorry. That is the only way I could prove my alibi."

Steve wrinkled his forehead. "Alibi for what?"

"Do you remember that woman who drives the fancy Jaguar who was here yesterday?"

He nodded. "Yeah, I remember... the crazy woman."

Simon shifted his weight. "This woman has accused me of killing her husband. Apparently, he was murdered around the time I was attending your neighborhood event last night. She told the police she spotted my car in their driveway around that same time, which of course is impossible, since it was parked in my driveway, while I was in your front yard."

Steve's eyes lit up. "Wow, that's incredible. Why

would she accuse you of being the murderer?"

Simon shrugged. "Maybe because she is the murderer and wanted to pin it on me. She even told the police I hit on her last night because I was infatuated with her."

"I'm assuming you weren't infatuated with her."

He shook his head. "Of course not. I do believe, though, she's dangerous."

Steve glanced at his watch. "I better get home and try and get a little sleep. I've had enough excitement for one night."

As he was about to shut the door, Simon said, "Thank you, Steve, for having an event tonight. Otherwise, I would have probably been spending the night in jail."

Steve waved, acknowledging he had heard him but did not respond.

Chapter 18

At 2:30 pm Thursday afternoon, the door opened from the hallway into the reception area of Simon's office.

A man's voice said, "Mr. Steed."

Simon rushed out of his office. Detective Williams stood in the middle of the reception area. His eyes darted around the room.

"Hello, Detective. How can I help you?"

"You've got a nice quaint office here."

Simon cocked his head. "Thank you."

The detective then stared at Simon. "You have a few minutes to talk?"

Simon gestured toward his office. "Yes, please come into my office and have a seat."

Detective Williams slid into one of the client chairs, and Simon sat behind his desk.

The detective's eyes scanned the room as he spoke. "As I said last night, you're not a suspect in the Steele case. But I still consider you a person of interest."

Simon stiffened, listening. "Yes, I understood that."

Detective Williams leaned back in his chair. "I spent the morning with Forensics at the Steeles residence. Based on what was discovered, I just want to tie up some loose ends. To expedite matters, I was hoping I could get your cooperation without the need of obtaining a search warrant."

Simon narrowed his eyes. "What kind of cooperation are you talking about?"

"I want you to come down to the station so we can get a sample of your DNA. It would help rule you out as anyway connected to this case."

Simon leaned forward. "Detective, I seriously doubt if you could get a judge to issue a warrant. The only evidence you have tying me to the scene of the crime is an eyewitness of a sick woman who told you she saw my car in her driveway last night. That has already been disproven."

Detective Williams sneered. "Does that mean that you aren't going to cooperate?"

"To be honest detective, under the same circumstances, I would advise my client not to agree to the DNA sample. However, I want to get this out of my hair. So, yes, I'll cooperate. When do I need to come down to the station?"

Detective Williams cracked a smile. "No time like the present."

Simon sighed. "I had a feeling you were going to say that."

"Do you know where the police department is located?"

Simon smirked. "No, I've never had the pleasure of going there."

Detective Williams grabbed the arm rest on his chair to support himself as he stood up. "4700 Drexel Drive. Do you need directions?"

Simon shook his head. "No, I am somewhat familiar with the area. I went to law school over at SMU. I can manage to find it."

Detective Williams fished in his coat pocket and pulled out a business card. "Give this to the receptionist and tell her you're there to see Sergeant Lewis."

Simon stood up and took the card. "I'll pack up my things and get right over there."

Detective Williams cock his head. "I hope this is the last time our paths will cross Mr. Steed."

"Me too."

* * *

Simon found a parking place just across from the Highland Park Police Station. A beautiful building with a Mediterranean style architecture façade, it did not resemble any police station he had seen in the past.

He opened the front door and spotted a woman sitting behind an ornate desk. Several uniformed police officers were milling around in the immediate area.

She looked up when he approached her. "May I help you?"

Simon handed her Detective Williams' business card. "May I see a Sergeant Lewis?"

The woman glanced down at the card and picked up the phone receiver and dialed a number. After a few seconds she said, "Sergeant Lewis, you have a visitor in the lobby. He gave me Detective Williams' card... Okay, I'll tell him."

She looked up at him. "Sergeant Lewis said for you to have a seat and he'll be down in a few minutes."

Simon sat down in the small reception area consisting of two chairs and an end table nestled between them. He kept his eyes on the elevator and staircase to his right. He wondered exactly how this would all play out. Ten minutes passed before a stocky, bald uniformed police officer descended the stairs and marched over to where Simon was sitting.

He said, "You must be Mr. Steed, I'm Sergeant Lewis."

Simon nodded. "Yes, that's me." He scrambled to his feet.

Sergeant Lewis gestured toward the stairs. "We will collect the DNA sample in the lab on the third floor. You don't mind if we take the stairs, do you?"

"No, that's fine."

Simon pondered why Sergeant Lewis opted for the stairs since he was panting by the time they reached the third floor. He pointed to a room with the laminated word 'Lab' centered on the wooden door. Sergeant Lewis pulled a set of keys out of his pocket and unlocked the door. Inside the room was an examination table, a small desk, two chairs, and a roll of lockers.

"You can sit on the edge of the examination table," Sergeant Lewis said. "The nurse will be here in a moment to draw the sample."

A thin, brunette mid-thirties woman wearing scrubs entered the room. She made a beeline to a box of plastic gloves sitting on the desk. Simon watched as she slipped on the gloves and removed a plastic bag and a sealed swab from the desk drawer.

Sergeant Lewis said, "This is Ms. Jane Connors. She's a registered nurse."

Jane smiled as she unsealed the swab. "I'm going to scrap the swab around the inside of your left cheek a few times. Please open your mouth and remain as still as possible."

After Jane drew the sample, she placed it in a plastic bag and sealed it with a sticker. She pulled a pen out of her pocket and put her initials on the seal. She handed the bag and pen to Simon.

"Please initial the sticker below my initials."

Simon did as he was instructed. He surmised that Jane was making certain no chain of custody issues would arise if she were ever called to testify in court. She unlocked one of the cabinets and placed the DNA sample inside and relocked the cabinet.

Simon said, "Is that it?"

Sergeant Lewis shook his head. "No, I need to get a set of your fingerprints. We'll do that over at the desk."

He had Simon place the tips of his fingers onto the surface of an ink pad and then press them down on a sheet of paper that had the image of an outline of a hand. After he completed the process, Sergeant Lewis handed him a wet cloth to clean the ink off his fingers. "Now you're free to go."

Simon thought about going back to his office, but he opted to drive home. As he was driving, he kept replaying the events of the last few days. Simon felt mentally and physically exhausted. Traffic was heavy as rush hour was soon approaching. He reached his home at last around 5:30 pm. As soon as Simon was inside his house, he went straight to the refrigerator and pulled out a can of Coors Light beer.

He decided to relax in his living room and listen to some music. When Simon opened the lid to his console, he groaned. Side 3 of the Beatles *White Album* was still resting on the turntable.

I'm not about to listen to Sexy Sadie tonight! I may never listen to that side of the album ever again!

He flipped through his collection of albums and pulled out The Cure's Seventeen Seconds album that was released a few years ago in 1980. Simon set the needle on the vinyl surface and plopped down in his overstuffed chair. He took several swigs of beer and closed his eyes. His peace was shattered by the sound of his doorbell. Simon peered through the peephole and saw Steve Paxton standing on his front porch.

He swung open the door. "Hey Steve. Would you like to come inside?"

Steve shook his head. "No, I just wanted you to know I spotted that fancy Jaguar on our street this afternoon."

Simon's eyes widened. "Seriously? Are you sure it was the same car?"

He nodded. "I'm positive! I know my cars. When I was coming home from work, I saw the Jaguar parked two houses down near where the Silks live. When I pulled in my driveway, I saw a truck parked in front of your house. I hurried inside and looked out my front living room window. A man and a woman stood on your front porch. The man appeared to be kneeling near your front door. I couldn't tell exactly what he was doing because the woman was positioned behind him which blocked my view."

Simon knelt and examined the doorknob and bolt lock. "Everything looks all right to me. What did the woman look like?"

"I could only see her from the back. She was a tall thin woman with dark hair."

Simon stood back up. "Do you remember how she was dressed?"

Steve shrugged. "Not, really. I think she was wearing a pantsuit of some sort. Women's fashion isn't really my thing."

Simon said, "I wonder if they were trying to pick my lock?"

"If they were trying to pick your lock, they weren't successful, because I watched until they finally left."

Simon gestured his head to the right. "Did you see

the woman get back into the Jaguar?"

Steve shook his head. "No, I can't see that far down the street from my front window. She did walk off in that direction, though. I watched the guy get into the truck."

"Was there any signage on the truck?"

"No, it was an old green Ford pickup. But there was no signage. Well, I better go. I'm going to be late for dinner."

Simon sighed. "Thank you for letting me know about the man and woman."

As he walked down the sidewalk Steve called out, "Be careful, Simon."

Chapter 19

Monday morning, Simon prepared to attend a hearing for a motion he had submitted to suppress evidence for a client in Judge Bonham's District Court. He was certain his motion would be denied, but it would provide him an opportunity to get some informal discovery of the prosecutor's case, should the matter go to trial.

Simon grabbed a quick lunch at the Record Grill in downtown Dallas. It was an informal greasy spoon diner frequented by attorneys. He got back to his office at 1:15 pm. When Simon reached his office, the door to his office was slightly ajar. He could have sworn he had locked it before he left for the courthouse this morning. Simon gave the door a slight push. He froze when he spotted Detective Williams sitting in a chair in his office reception area.

Detective Williams stood up when Simon entered the room. "In case you're wondering how I got in your office; the building manager unlocked it for me."

Simon took a deep breath to calm his nerves. "Am I being arrested?"

The detective shook his head. "Not yet. But I need you to come down to the station for questioning."

Simon dropped his briefcase. "Are you going to handcuff me?"

"I will spare you that, if you voluntarily come with me to the station."

Neither man spoke as they drove north to Highland Park. Simon kept pondering what evidence the police could possibly have to want to question him any further about Sterling Steele's homicide. Detective Williams parked in his reserved parking place near the rear entrance to the Highland Park Police Station at 4700 Drexel Drive.

As they walked into the building, Simon felt as if everyone was staring at him, trying to figure out why he was with Detective Williams. They took the elevator to the second floor.

As soon as they exited the elevator, Detective Williams gestured with his head. "This way."

Simon followed him down a narrow hallway lined with wood doors. The detective stopped at a door midway down the hall. Next to the door was a laminated sign containing the words 'Interrogation Room 1'.

Detective Williams opened the door. He pointed at a wooden chair situated behind a table at the end of the small room. "Sit in that chair and I'll be back in a minute."

Simon did as the detective had instructed. He plopped down and surveyed his surroundings. The ceiling, walls, and floor of the narrow room were a faded beige color. A table was situated in the center of the room with three chairs around it, two on one side, one on the other. In the center of the table sat a tape recorder.

Simon could not help but recognize the resemblance this room had to the room at Parkland Behavior Health Center where a doctor had interviewed him before he was allowed to be discharged from inpatient care. The same thoughts kept running through his head as to why the police needed to question him further.

Ten minutes later, the door opened, and Detective Williams and another man entered the room.

Detective Williams said, "This is Detective John Jamison."

Detective Jamison was a mid-thirties, dark-headed man with chiseled features. He was dressed in a charcoal gray suit, blue tie, and white shirt. Both men sat down across the table from Simon.

Detective Williams switched on the tape recorder and adjusted the small microphone, so it was aimed at Simon. He said, "As I have informed you, Mr. Steed, you are not yet under arrest. However, I'm still going to give you the Miranda Warning. You have the right to remain silent. Anything you say can and will be used against you in a court of law. You have the right to an attorney. If you cannot afford an attorney, one will be provided for you."

Simon surmised the detective had given the Miranda Warning countless times during his career.

Detective Williams said, "Have you ever had the

occasion to be inside the Steele residence on Beverly Drive?"

Simon paused to collect his thoughts before answering. He nodded. "Yes, I have been there one time."

Both detectives' eyes were laser focused on him. "Do you remember the date?"

Simon glanced up at the ceiling. "Let's see. It was a week ago last Saturday. Mrs. Steele asked me to come to her house. We had—"

Detective Williams said, "She asked you to come to her house?"

Simon nodded. "That's correct. As I was about to say, we had a hearing scheduled for Monday morning. I had spent Saturday morning in my office going through records provided by her husband's attorney pursuant to a subpoena duces tecum."

Detective Jamison chimed in. "Why didn't she come to your office? Wouldn't that have made more sense?"

Simon shifted in his chair. "Yes, that was my preference, but she insisted that I come to her house."

Detective Williams leaned forward. "Was Mr. Steele there at the time?"

"No, she said he was out of town."

Both detectives glanced at each other.

"What time did you go to her house?" Detective Williams said.

Simon rubbed his nose. "I got there a bit early and parked across the street. I was going to wait until

5:00 pm before going up to ring the doorbell. As I was sitting there, I spotted Mrs. Steele talking to a man I recognized. The same man just showed up one day in my office and said he was friends with the Steeles. He was less than subtle by insisting that the divorce be concluded amicably and as soon as possible."

Detective Jamison said, "What do you mean by 'less than subtle'?"

Simon bounced. "He told me to accept the settlement offer made by Rowan Stedman, her husband's attorney. I told him I was going to represent the best interests of my client. He then made a point of making sure I knew he was carrying a pistol and said he would be returning to Oak Cliff."

Detective Williams said, "Did this man tell you, his name?"

Simon nodded. "Yes, he said his name was Boris Denucci."

Detective Williams cleared his throat. "So, you're waiting across the street. What happened next?"

"After a few minutes, this Denucci character got in his car, backed out of her driveway, and drove off. That's when I saw the red lights of a police car in my rearview mirror. Apparently, one of the neighbors called 911, saying they saw a suspicious car parked near their house. I drive an old Pontiac, so I can understand why they were suspicious."

Detective Williams said, "Did the officer question you?"

"Yes, he asked me what I was doing there, and I told him that I was an attorney and had a meeting with Mrs. Steele on a legal matter. The officer then asked to see my bar card. When I showed it to him, he seemed satisfied with everything."

Detective Jamison said, "Do you recall the officer's name?"

Simon sighed and closed his eyes. "Let me think about it. Yes, I remember now, it was Officer Daniels."

Detective Williams said, "Frank Daniels?"

Simon shrugged. "I don't recall his first name."

Detective Williams tapped the table with his palm. "Go on with your story."

"Well, I grabbed my box of records and went up to the house. Mrs. Steele led me to a room that she described as her workroom. She asked if I would like a glass of wine because she was going to have a glass and didn't want to drink alone. After she returned with a bottle of chardonnay and two glasses of wine, we went through the records to prepare for the hearing."

Detective Jamison leaned forward. "Do you usually drink alcohol while meeting with your clients."

Simon snickered. "No, that's the first time."

Detective Williams shifted in his chair. "How did the meeting with her go?"

"It went fine. I found what I thought was an omission in the records provided, which she then confirmed. I could tell by her body language that she was terribly angry with her husband. Mrs. Steele told me she hated him and wished she possessed the same powers as me. She said if she did have these powers, she would kill him. Then she went on to say she hoped her husband would provoke me so that I would cause his death."

Detective Jamison cocked his head. "What are these powers you possess?"

Before Simon could respond, Detective Williams said, "Mr. Steed thinks he has telepathic powers to wreak havoc on anyone who provokes him. Is that an accurate description?"

Simon nodded. "Yes, that's pretty accurate. It has happened several times in my life. But none since I've had therapy and medication."

Detective Jamison rolled his eyes. "So, Mrs. Steele wanted her husband to provoke these powers in you since she was not capable of doing it, correct?"

Simon grimaced. "That's correct."

Detective Williams leaned forward. "Would these powers include you shooting him with a pistol?"

Simon emphatically shook his head. "No, absolutely not! That's not how it works. I'm not physically involved in the demise of individuals who provoke me. It's mental telepathy."

The detectives glanced again at one another. Detective Williams said, "Did Mr. Steele ever provoke you?"

Simon nodded. "Yes, right after the hearing the following Monday. He was furious because I provided enough evidence for the judge to rule against his motion. After the hearing, he threatened me just outside of the courtroom and even grabbed the lapels of my coat jacket. I thought he was going to hit me, but his attorney intervened and got him to calm down."

Detective Williams' eyes widened. "Because of this angry outburst on his part, you could cause something bad to happen to him?"

Simon shrugged. "I remember thinking as he walked away, that prior to my treatment at Parkland Behavior Health Center and being on medication, I probably would have been provoked. But I did nothing."

Detective Williams said, "Mr. Steed. The night that Mr. Steele was murdered, two wine glasses were found in the kitchen. One glass had the fingerprints of the deceased, and the other glass had your fingerprints. I know of your alibi at the time a shot was heard by the neighbors but were you there earlier in the day?"

Simon held his palms up. "The only time that I was ever in that house was that Saturday to discuss the records with Mrs. Steele. Don't you think Mrs. Steele might have saved the glass I used from that meeting to set me up as the culprit?"

Detective Jamison growled, "That assumes your story about being there for a meeting was the truth."

Simon slammed a fist onto the table. "It is, damn it. Can't you check with Officer Daniels?"

Detective Williams said, "Settle down. We, of course, will check your story out with the officer. But he didn't give you a ticket, did he?"

"No, I told you he said I was free to go after seeing my bar card."

Detective Williams rubbed his chin. "The officers have a lot of encounters with people every day. Unless they write someone a ticket or arrest someone, they may not remember every encounter. Did anything happen during your conversation with him that might jar his memory?"

Simon nodded. "Yes, he will surely remember my car. As you know, I drive a 1966 Pontiac Lemans. He commented that the neighbors probably thought I was suspicious because 1960s vintage cars are not usually seen in the neighborhood. Also, he noted the zip code on my driver's license was 75224, which is in the heart of Oak Cliff."

Detective Williams narrowed his eyes. "Do you own a gun of any type?"

Simon shook his head. "No, I haven't owned a gun since I was twelve years old. My dad gave me a 410-shotgun on my birthday. I may have fired it once or twice but never went hunting or anything. I sold the gun in a garage sale when I became an adult."

Detective Jamison said, "Have you ever shot a pistol of any sort?"

"No, never. I don't like guns of any kind. I wouldn't even know how to load one."

Detective Williams said, "Mrs. Steele told us she called 911 when she found her husband lying in a pool of blood in the kitchen. She said she panicked because she didn't know if the killer might still be in the house. She switched on the front porch light, opened the front door, and started to run over to her neighbor's house to wait for the police to arrive. That's when she spotted the pistol partially concealed in the bushes next to the sidewalk. No one touched it until Forensics arrived on the scene."

Simon sat still, listening intently to the detective. He was careful not to change expressions. He assumed they were trying to see if he showed any emotion when hearing about the pistol that was found at the scene of the crime.

"A small Smith & Wesson 340PD." Detective Jamison leaned forward. "Ever seen that type of pistol?"

Simon shook his head. "No, I don't think so. I've heard of the brand Smith & Wesson, but I don't know anything else about them."

Detective Williams said, "Forensics said a faint print found on the handle of the pistol was remarkably like one of your fingerprints. The expert who conducted the examination indicated it was not one hundred percent conclusive. He said if he were a betting man, however, he would claim it was a match."

Simon sneered. "That can't be possible. I…I…" He bolted upright, his eyes wide. "Wait a damn minute. That could be my fingerprint on the pistol."

Detective Williams' eyes lit up. "Go on."

Simon bounced in his chair. "A couple of weeks ago, I was assaulted in my driveway when I got home one night from work. Someone hit me on the back of the head, and I crumpled to the ground. I pretended to be unconscious. I didn't want the assailant to keep beating me, because I assumed I was being robbed and the assailant was just after my wallet. What was strange is that a gloved hand lifted my right hand off the ground and squeezed it around something hard. The next thing I heard were footsteps running away down my driveway. When I was able to sit up, I fished in my coat pocket for my wallet, and to my surprise it was still there."

Lacing his fingers together, Detective Williams said, "So then what?"

"I bet you anything Veronica Steele hired Boris Denucci to get my fingerprints on the pistol. She had hoped she could convince me to use my powers to kill her husband. If that failed, she was going to use my fingerprints on the pistol and wine glass to set me up as the murderer."

Anger stirred inside Simon, like fire in his gut, as he pondered what he had just said.

Detective Jamison said, "Did you report this assault to the police?"

Simon shook his head. "No, since I wasn't robbed, I just let it go."

Detective Jamison frowned. "Did anyone else witness the assault?"

Simon considered mentioning that Raven saw his body lying on the driveway from her bedroom window but doubted now if she even existed. "I don't think so."

Detective Williams said, "Did you tell anyone about this assault?"

Simon shook his head again. "No. Let me ask you detectives, has the Highland Park Police conducted a thorough search of the entire Steele residence for evidence, or did you just reach the conclusion I was the culprit. Don't you think it was convenient that Veronica Steele happened to see the pistol in the front hedges and that her husband had a glass of wine with the killer? If I killed Mr. Steele, do you think I'd be foolish enough to leave my fingerprints on not only the pistol but also an empty wine glass?"

Detective Williams sneered. "I'm not going to reveal the specifics of any type of the investigation."

"Detectives, if you conduct a thorough search of the Steele residence, it's possible you will find the evidence you need to tie Veronica Steele to the murder of her husband."

Detective Williams turned toward Detective Jamison. "Detective, do you have any further questions?"

He shook his head a third time. "No."

Detective Williams leaned across the table to where the tape recorder was situated and switched it off. He glanced up at Simon. "You sit here. We're going to go run your story by Officer Daniels."

Simon sat still and watched as the two detectives exited the room, locking the door behind them. He replayed the whole interrogation back through his head.

Do they have probable cause to arrest me? He tapped his forefinger on the edge of the table. *Perhaps, but it's obviously not ironclad or otherwise I would already be locked up. God, I hope that officer remembers me being in Highland Park that day.*

Simon stared at the door, waiting to find out his fate. At last, thirty minutes later, someone unlocked the door and Detective Williams swung it open. "You're fortunate Officer Daniels' has a photographic memory. At this point, you're not under arrest, at least for the moment. I'll take you back to your office."

Simon breathed a sigh of relief.

Detective Williams pulled up to the curb at the side of the Oak Cliff Bank tower. As Simon opened the door, he said, "Thank you for not arresting me."

Detective Williams glared at him. "In my younger days, you would be behind bars based on this evidence. But since I became a detective, I make damn sure all my ducks are in order in a case. I don't want some half-ass criminal lawyer getting you off on a technicality."

Simon shut the door without responding.

Chapter 20

Monday afternoon, Simon glanced at his wristwatch. It was 5:30 pm. He was tired and decided to go home. He turned right onto Woolsey Drive and drove down the street toward his house.

When Simon was about fifty feet away, he spotted the taillights of a car in front of his house. Once he pulled within a few yards, the car squealed away from the curb and sped down his street in the opposite direction.

Simon could not get a good look at the car in the darkness. The last thing he wanted tonight was any more excitement.

Simon spent the night watching television. He stumbled across an old Sherlock Holmes movie on Channel 11. After the movie, Simon flipped off the television and walked over to the window.

As he had routinely done, he cracked open the venetian blinds and peer out at his neighbor's windows. Simon spotted through the sheer curtains the silhouette of a female pacing back in forth in her bedroom. He rubbed his head.

How can that be Raven? The house is supposed to be vacant. I saw the lockbox myself.

Simon jolted at the sound of his doorbell ringing. He closed the blinds and hurried through the dark house toward the front door in his living room.

Who the hell is ringing my doorbell this time of night?

Simon switched on the front porch light peered out through the peephole.

His eyes widened when he saw Raven standing in the middle of the porch.

What's Raven doing here when I just saw her silhouette seconds ago in her bedroom?

Simon cracked open the door. "Raven?"

The same as when he first met her, she was wearing a blue shirt, blue jeans, and flats. Her piercing green eyes sparkled from the front porch light. She cracked a half smile. "Hello Simon, may I come in?"

He swung the door wide open. "Uh, sure, is everything okay?"

As Raven stepped inside his living room, her eyes darted around. She walked over to his console and lifted the lid and glanced at the turntable. "I see Side 3. of the Beatles *White Album* is no longer on the turntable."

Simon narrowed his eyes. "No, I haven't listened to that album for a while. Would you care to sit down?"

"Yes, thank you." She walked over and perched

on the middle of the sofa. He plopped down in the overstuffed chair nearby.

Simon said, "May I ask you a question?"

Raven flipped her brown hair over her shoulder. "Fire away."

He leaned forward. "You don't live next door, do you?"

She snickered.

Simon cocked his head. "What's so funny?"

Raven batted her eyelashes. "If you don't think I live next door, then why do you stare at me out of your den window almost every night?"

He sank into his chair as his face blushed. "You've seen me?"

She cackled. "Of course, I've seen you. In fact, I wanted you to watch me."

Simon wrinkled his forehead. "You wanted me to watch you? Why?"

Raven cracked an incredulous smile. "I wanted to remain front and center of your attention. The more you think about me, the stronger I become."

He held up the palms of his hands. "I... I don't understand."

She shifted her weight on the sofa. "It's difficult adapting to that strong medication you're taking for Dissociative Identity Disorder."

Simon was now laser focused on her. "How did you know about my mental illness?"

Raven smiled. "You're not getting it yet, are you? Did you think Monica disappeared after you went inpatient at Parkland Behavior Health Center? Your therapy and medication were extremely effective, but the will to survive is extraordinarily strong, regardless of how many mutations I must experience."

He shook his head, as if trying to fling off some small animal clutching his hair. "No-no-no, that's not possible. You want me to believe you're a variant of Monica?"

She winked at him. "Bingo! I aspire to be your dominant personality."

Simon's skin turned clammy, and his heart raced. "I can't and don't believe you."

Raven bounced on the sofa. "Okay, I'll convince you. Does the name Betsy Browning sound familiar?"

He rubbed his forehead. "Betsy Browning?"

"You remember, the cute smart girl in your sixth-grade class."

Simon nodded. "Yes, she lived behind me one house down to the left."

She smiled. "What kind of dog did you have when you were in the sixth grade?"

"A beagle. Just like my neighbor Ted Clements had when he came to my door accusing me of calling him about his barking dog."

Raven stroked her dark hair. "Remember when someone would call in the middle of the night to complain that your family's beagle's barking was disturbing them? But the person would whisper, and your father couldn't tell who was calling."

He sighed. "Yes, the caller would whisper, 'quiet

your barking dog, and then hang up. Just like the calls that I've been receiving. We never knew who was calling, until one day, Betsy let it slip that my dog was keeping her awake at night."

Raven chuckled. "That's correct and you solved the mystery for the family."

Simon nodded. "Yes, one of the few bright spots of my childhood."

She smiled. "Believe me now?"

He frowned. "Does Ted Clements even exist?"

Raven stood up. "What you think is all that matters. Stay safe, Simon, I need you to stay alive. I have big plans for us."

He edged forward to stand up and she motioned with her right hand for him to remain seated. "Keep your seat, I'll see myself out."

Simon sat motionless and watched her glide across the living room, open the door, and exit the house. He thought about sprinting over to the living room window to watch her walk away but decided she had probably vanished.

What the hell just happened? Am I hallucinating again like I did before I went inpatient? He sat up straight. *Did I kill Sterling Steele? Does he or Veronica Steele even exist? What about Detective Williams? Who exists and doesn't exist?*

Simon walked back into his den and opened the venetian blinds. He stared at his next door neighbor's house. All the windows were pitch black. Simon went into his kitchen and grabbed the phone receiver off the cradle on the wall dialed a number. He listened as the phone rang on the other end of the line.

The recorded voice at the other end of the line said, "This is Dr. Roberts. Please leave your message at the sound of the tone and I'll return your call as soon as possible. If this is an emergency, hang up and dial 911."

After the sound of the tone, Simon said, "Dr. Roberts, this is Simon Steed, I'm experiencing hallucinations. May I please make an appointment to come to see you as soon as possible? You have my home and office phone numbers. Thank you."

Chapter 21

On Tuesday morning, Simon arrived at his office at 9:00 am. He had trouble falling asleep Monday night and slept in late. Simon needed to prepare some motions for clients but could not concentrate. He stared blank-faced out his office window, thinking about Raven. Simon jolted when the phone on his desk rang.

He answered after the second ring. "Hello, this is Simon Steed."

A woman's voice said, "Mr. Steed, please hold for Dr. Roberts."

A few seconds later, a man's voice said, "Mr. Steed, this is Dr. Roberts. I got your message. Tell me about these hallucinations you said you were experiencing."

Simon sighed. "They're remarkably like what I experienced prior to going inpatient at the hospital. Do you remember me telling you about Monica, the girl I met in college?"

"Of course, I reviewed your file before calling you. Has she returned?"

Simon frowned. "In a sense, yes. This woman is named Raven instead, but she told me she's a variant of Monica."

Dr. Roberts rustled papers. "Did this Raven just appear out of the blue and claim to be a variant of Monica?"

He shook his head. "No, she first appeared after I was released from Parkland. She posed as my next door neighbor."

"Does she look like Monica?"

Simon leaned back in his chair. "No, Raven is also beautiful, but looks different than Monica. Anyway, she said she thought my house was vacant. When Raven saw my lights on, she came over to introduce herself. I soon discovered that at night, I could see her silhouette through the sheer curtains in her bedroom. When Raven came over last night, she revealed she aspires to be my dominant personality. She also told me she knew I had been looking at her in the bedroom. That was her plan. The more I thought about her, the stronger she became."

Dr. Roberts heaved a big sigh. "Did Raven ever make an appearance when anyone else was around?"

Simon shifted in his chair. "No, no one in the neighborhood knew anything about her. The house next door, where she said she lived, is vacant. One of my neighbors told me it was tied up in an estate dispute."

"Okay, Mr. Steed, I'm going to have my assistant contact you in a few minutes to schedule an appointment for you. In the meantime, I'll call in a prescription of risperidone to your pharmacy. Take it with all your other medications. It will be a day or two before you feel the effects, but you should be fine until you come to my office for your appointment."

* * *

Simon stopped by Craven's Pharmacy on Zang Boulevard in Oak Cliff to pick up his prescription. As soon as he climbed back into his Pontiac, he read the directions on the prescription bottle's label and right away swallowed a tablet. Simon took a deep breath. He was thankful he had contacted the doctor and was being proactive with his medical care.

Simon turned right onto Woolsey Drive from Shelmire and wound his way down his street toward his house. He hit the brakes in front of his next door neighbor's house. A Mercedes SUV and a Toyota SUV were parked in front of the house. Simon surmised a realtor was showing the house to potential buyers.

He pulled into his driveway and turned off the engine. He made his way to the front porch and unlocked the front door.

As Simon stepped into his living room, he heard a scratching sound. He dropped his briefcase by the door and walked over to his console where he heard the source of the noise. Simon gasped when he looked down and saw the needle of his turntable skipping at the end of Side 3. of the Beatles' *White Album*. A chill shot down his spine.

Who is here? Why is this happening? Is it Raven?

Does it have to do with Sexy Sadie?

Simon lifted the needle off the record, turned off the console, and slipped the album into the dust cover. His eyes darted around. He trembled as he went through every room in his house, searching every nook and cranny. Simon expected that any second someone might leap at him out of a hiding place.

His bedroom was the only room left to search. He took care as he opened the bedroom door and switched on the light. Everything looked as it did when he left this morning.

Still cautious, Simon opened his closet door and peered inside. Nothing appeared out of the ordinary. He took several deep beaths out of relief.

Simon scrambled back to his kitchen. He needed a drink to help calm his nerves. Simon swung open the refrigerator door and froze. A shattered empty Flowers Chardonnay wine bottle was spread out covering the entire top shelf of his refrigerator.

Who did this? Why?

He stood and stared at the shattered bottle. He remembered that Veronica Steele had served him a glass of Flowers Chardonnay when he met with her at her house.

Veronica must have broken into my house! She wanted to leave enough hints, so I knew she was here and wanted me to feel vulnerable! He glanced in both directions. *She's succeeded!*

Simon sprinted through his house, making sure

all the doors were locked and the windows secured. He considered calling the police, but nothing was stolen from his house, and he had no visible evidence that anyone broke in.

He couldn't settle down. Simon jumped every time he thought he heard some kind of noise.

He fixed a quick dinner and ate it while watching television. Simon stayed tuned to it straight through until 10:00 pm and then turned it off. He flipped on the front porch and back porch lights and made the rounds, rechecking all the doors and windows. Fully clothed at 10:45 pm, Simon at last climbed into bed.

At midnight, he jolted and sat up straight in bed. *What's that noise?*

Simon switched on the lamp next to the bed and blinked several times, allowing his eyes to adjust to the light. What sounded like faint music came from the front of his house.

When he cracked open his bedroom door, the music grew louder. Simon's palms turned clammy as he made his way down the hallway to the side entrance to his living room.

As he poked his head around the door frame, the song, Everybody's Got Something to Hide played from Side 3. of the Beatles *White Album*. The living room was dark except for the glow created by the console.

A female voice said, "You're just in time, Simon."

He flinched as he recognized Veronica Steele's voice. She switched on the lamp on the table next to the sofa. She was dressed head-to-toe in black, perched on the edge of the sofa. In her right hand was a small pistol aimed in his direction.

He screamed, "How the hell did you get in?"

Veronica flashed an incredulous smile. "Elementary, my dear Simon." She opened the palm of her left hand. "I let myself in the front door."

His mouth dropped open. "How did you get a key?"

"I met a locksmith here one day and he made me a lovely key." She snickered. "Don't you like the color red? It matches my nails perfectly. Please sit down, Simon. You're making me nervous, standing there trembling."

He stumbled over to the overstuffed chair and plopped down. "What do you want from me?"

Veronica sneered. "This isn't a social call. I don't know what lies you told the Highland Park Police, but they got a warrant to search my home. Simon, you know very well you killed Sterling! You were so infatuated with me."

"I... I didn't kill him. Sexy Sadie killed him, didn't she, Veronica?"

"But your fingerprints were on the wine glass," she growled, "and on the pistol!"

Simon felt more emboldened. "You set me up as the murderer. You served me wine at your house so you could use my fingerprints from the glass. Then, you had that gorilla, Boris Denucci, assault me in the driveway to get my prints on the pistol, isn't that right, Sadie? You even had Deloris, the bartender, pose as Margot when I called the number on the matchbox. That's right, I finally remember now where I heard her voice before. You thought that might help provoke me to kill your husband."

Her lips pursed and her face was drawn. Veronica suddenly cast a glance over at the console and jerked her head back around to face him. She raised the pistol up to her lips and whispered, "Shhh. It's on next."

After a few seconds of pops and crackles, the song, 'Sexy Sadie', played on the album. Veronica pointed the pistol at him and closed her eyes.

Simon was laser focused on her, trying to anticipate her next move. Was she going to kill him after the song? He pondered whether he should rush her while her eyes were closed and attempt to knock the pistol out of her hand.

As he was about to spring out of the chair, he spotted some movement on his front porch through a crack in the curtains. A uniformed police officer looked in through the window.

Simon pointed over to where Veronica sat. He watched as the police officer craned his neck so he could see where he was pointing.

John Lennon sang the final line in the song,

However big you think you are.

The music faded out and Veronica opened her eyes. She sneered and squinted at him.

Both jumped at the pounding on the front door.

A voice from outside shouted, "Open the door! Dallas Police Department!"

Veronica glanced back around at Simon.

He murmured, "Veronica, let me open the door."

Tears welled up in her eyes as she nodded.

Simon raced to the front door and yanked it open. "Thank God, you're here!"

Two cautious Dallas police officers entered with their pistols drawn. Simon glanced over at Veronica. Her head hung down toward her chest and the pistol dangled in her right hand.

One of the officers shouted, "Drop the weapon!"

She raised her head while dropping the pistol at the same time.

The officer kicked it out of her reach. He then picked up the pistol. "I'm Officer Davenport and she's Officer Edwards. Who are you?"

Veronica's face contorted. "Sadie," she hissed.

"Do you have a last name, Sadie?"

Simon said, "Officer, her name is Veronica Steele."

Officer Davenport pointed down at her handbag sitting next to her on the floor. "Ma'am, is that your handbag? May I see your driver's license?"

Veronica sat motionless, staring blank-faced ahead. Officer Davenport picked up her handbag, removed her wallet, and pulled out her driver's license. He studied it for a few seconds.

"Ms. Steele, what are doing over here in this part of town tonight with a pistol?"

She didn't move and didn't answer.

"Officer," Simon said, "she's mentally ill. I'm not sure she knows what she's doing."

Even under the circumstances, he could not help but see the irony in his telling the officers about her mental illness.

Officer Davenport placed handcuffs on Veronica and the officers led her out of the house.

His neighbor, Steve, appeared at the open front door. "Everything okay, Simon?"

Simon took a deep breath. "I think so."

"When I spotted the lady's Jaguar parked in your driveway," Steve said, "I decided to call the police. I thought something bad might be happening over here."

Simon nodded. "You're right about that. By the way, what are you doing up so late at night?"

He sighed. "My flight was delayed, and I just got home from DFW Airport."

Simon patted him on the shoulder. "I'm glad your flight was delayed or tonight may have had a different outcome."

Chapter 22

Simon took the morning off. He did not arrive at his office until 1:00 pm. He was preparing for a trial when the door from the hallway to his reception area opened. Simon dropped his pen on the desk and hurried over to his office door. His face dropped.

Detective Williams stood there with his hands folded. He appeared to be examining a piece of artwork on the wall.

Without looking at Simon, he said, "What's the story behind the framed crime tape? That's not the type of art one usually sees in an office."

Simon took a deep breath to calm his nerves. "It's from an event that occurred when I was in high school. There's no significance. I just thought it would make a good conversation piece."

The detective turned around and looked at him. "If you say so. I can't say I've ever understood modern art."

"I suspect, detective, that you didn't come all the way over from Highland Park to discuss art."

Detective Williams chuckled. "You're right about that. Do you have a few minutes to visit?"

Simon gestured with his head toward his office. "Please come into my office."

The detective settled into one of Simon's client chairs and Simon into the chair behind his desk.

"I wanted to talk to you about the Steele case. We got a warrant and conducted a thorough search of the Steele residence."

Simon leaned forward. "I know, Veronica Steele told me last night."

The detective's eyes widened. "Really? How did that all come about?"

Simon sighed. "When I got home from work last evening, I noticed some strange things. First, my stereo console was turned on. The needle from the turntable was skipping at the end of one of the Beatles albums. That side of the album has some significance to Veronica which I will get to in a minute."

He paused and took a deep breath. "Anyway, I searched my house room by room, and didn't see anything out of order. After my investigation, I went into the kitchen to get a beer out of my refrigerator. On the top shelf of the refrigerator was a shattered bottle of Flowers Chardonnay. That's the same type of wine Veronica Steele served me at her house. I think she definitely wanted to scare me and make me feel vulnerable."

Detective Williams' gaze was focused on him. "Did you contact the Dallas Police?"

Simon shook his head. "No, I probably should have called them. The only precaution I took was to check and recheck all the doors and windows to make certain they were locked."

Detective Williams shifted in his chair. "You do like to live dangerously, don't you, Mr. Steed?"

Simon shrugged. "I suppose so. Anyway, after I went to bed, I was awakened around midnight by noise coming from my living room at the front of my house. As I drew nearer to the room, I recognized the noise was from Side 3. of the Beatles *White Album*. When I reached it, the only light inside the room was the glow from my stereo console."

"What happened next?"

"In the darkness, Veronica Steele said, 'You're just in time, Simon.' She then flipped on the lamp next to where she sat on the sofa. In her right hand, she held a pistol aimed in my direction."

Detective Williams said, "How did she get inside your house?"

"Veronica got a locksmith to make her a key. That's when she told me about the police getting a warrant to search her house. She then accused me again of murdering her husband since my fingerprints were on the wine glass and pistol handle. I told her I figured out her scheme of getting my fingerprints on the glass and having Boris Denucci assault me so he could get my fingerprints on the pistol, too. That's when I called her 'Sadie'."

Detective Williams cocked his head. "You lost me there. Why did you call her Sadie?"

Simon bounced in his chair. "Side 3. of the Beatles

White Album includes a song by John Lennon named 'Sexy Sadie'. I think one of Veronica's personalities is Sadie. The personality who killed her husband."

Despite his frowning, Detective Williams nodded.

"Veronica made us listen to the song. She seemed to go into a trance. I didn't know whether to try to wrestle the pistol out of her hand or sit still. I think she intended to shoot me after the song. As the song neared the end, I spotted a Dallas police officer peering into my living room through the front window. I pointed in Veronica's direction, hoping he would see she was armed with a pistol."

"And did he?"

"Yes. Right at the end of the song, the policeman pounded on the door. In a calm voice, I asked Veronica if I could let them in. To my surprise, she nodded. The police entered and took control of the situation. When they asked Veronica to state her name, she told them it was Sadie. One of the officers found her driver's license with her Highland Park address and asked her what she was doing in this part of town at that time of night. Veronica didn't respond. She appeared to be in some kind of trance again."

"How did the police know there might be a disturbance at your house?"

Simon stretched his neck. "My neighbor called them. He saw her Jaguar parked in my driveway. From an earlier incident, I had told him she was unusual and mentally unstable. Fortunately for me, he called them."

Detective Williams leaned back in his chair. "That's just the tip of the iceberg of the problems she's facing."

Simon's eyes lit up. "Did you find something to incriminate her in your search?"

He nodded. "Yep, we found a plastic glove hidden in a shoe in her closet. Forensics found gun powder residue and her fingerprints on them."

"So, is your investigation now complete?"

"Yes. Except for one thing and that's why I'm here. I wanted to apologize to you. I was a little hard on you."

Simon smiled. "Thank you, Detective."

The detective pushed down on the chair's armrests to help himself stand up. "Have a good day, Mr. Steed."

Simon stood and walked with him to the door leading to the hallway. "Goodbye detective."

* * *

After work, Simon decided he would celebrate by treating himself to some Tex-Mex food at El Fenix at the intersection of Colorado Boulevard and Zang Boulevard in Oak Cliff. He downed a generous plate of cheese enchiladas and two margaritas.

As Simon turned on Woolsey Drive, he slowed down in front of his next door neighbor's house. The realtor lock box was still secured on the front door handle and the For Sale sign still planted in the front lawn.

It will be nice to get some real neighbors sometime.

Simon changed into some comfortable clothes and settled into an evening of watching television. He found the 1950s movie, *A Creature from the Black Lagoon*, showing on Channel 11. He smiled as he remembered watching the same movie with his brother Steve one Saturday night during his childhood in the 1960s.

When the movie ended, he switched off the television and intended to walk back to the other side of the house to his bedroom. At the last second, he strolled over to the window in his den. Simon cracked open the venetian blinds and peeked at his neighbor's bedroom window.

His mouth dropped open when a silhouette figure appeared through the sheer draped curtains, standing still and staring at him. Right away he closed the blinds and shut his eyes.

All the good feelings of the day quickly dissipated! "Damn!"

ACKNOWLEDGMENTS

This is my sixth novel with Treaty Oak Publishers. Cynthia Stone always provides outstanding guidance through every phase of completing a book, from editing to cover design. I am very thankful to have her expertise throughout the whole process.

I would also like to thank Kimberly Greyer for her design work in bringing the cover to life.

ABOUT THE AUTHOR

After practicing law for many years, Jim decided to pursue his passion full time as a visual artist, film maker and author. He received the 2016 Merrimack Media Outstanding Writer Award for his second novel, *Punitive Damages*. *Arbitrary and Capricious* is the fourth novel in a series. *Choking on the Splinters* is the third novel in a series, a Global Book Bronze Award winner for Mystery and Suspense. *Surreal Absurdity*, also a Global Book Bronze Award winner, is a sequel to his novel, *Aberrant Behavior. Your Brain's Still Flashing* is a sequel to *Never Ignore Monica*, a finalist in the Thriller genre for the 2024 Book Excellence Awards.

His artwork and art films have been recognized in numerous juried competitions, publications and film festivals. He has exhibited his artwork in several group and solo exhibitions across North America and Europe.

Eighteen of Jim's films have been selected to various film festivals around the world. His art film, *The Soul of Vinyl, Abbey Road Side 2*. screened at the 2016 New York City Independent Film Festival. Jim's film, *The Case of the Deranged Sommelier*, won Best Experimental Film in the 2016 Directors Circle of Shorts Film Festival and the 2017 Lion's Head Film Festival. His film, *Still Mad as Hell*, screened at the 2017 New York City Independent Film Festival. His film, *It's Gonna Disappear*, screened at the 2021 New York Flash Film Festival. His latest film, *Top Secret and Not So Confidential*, was selected as a Semi-Finalist in the 2023 San Jose Independent Film Festival.

Jim's education includes a Bachelor of Arts from The University of Texas at Austin, a Juris Doctor from Southern Methodist University in Dallas, and Level One Wine Sommelier Certification from the International Wine and Spirits Guild.

His website is www.jimlivelyart.com.